"I granted you your fre
yet I ask you now, Gar
your promise to remain here as a valued member
of my family."

She pressed her hands together.

"Would you have me pray, or are you asking for time to pray, yourself?"

She scooted off the log and cast a look at the distance.

"Aye. Go and talk with the Lord. It is fitting to seek His wisdom in all things." Garnet disappeared behind a grove of trees, and Samuel turned his attention on the children. Ethan handed Hester a little boat he'd made from a bit of bark and a leaf. She squealed with joy and set it in the water. As it started to float, she wrapped her arms around Ethan's waist and hugged him. By the time she looked back, her boat had drifted out of reach. She let out a cry and started to go after it. For an instant, Samuel started to rise.

Christopher grabbed Hester by the waist and twirled her back onto dry land. "Let's go make more!"

Seeing Christopher attend Hester allowed Sam to sit back down. Garnet showed wisdom in seeking the Lord's will. Sam rubbed his hands on his knees again. *I'm never anxious, yet I'm even more nervous than when I asked Naomi to wed me. Naomi was a stranger to me; the widow abides beneath my roof and has proven to be of excellent character. She is kind beyond telling and holds great affection for the children. Surely that will sway her to make this commitment.*

But what if she doesn't?

CATHY MARIE HAKE is a Southern California native who loves her work as a nurse and Lamaze teacher. She and her husband have a daughter, a son, and three dogs, so life is never dull or quiet. Cathy considers herself a sentimental pack rat, collecting antiques and Hummel figurines. In spare moments, she reads, bargain hunts, and makes a huge mess with her new hobby of scrapbooking. cathy@cathymariehake.com

Books by Cathy Marie Hake

HEARTSONG PRESENTS
HP370—Twin Victories
HP481—Unexpected Delivery
HP512—Precious Burdens
HP545—Love Is Patient
HP563—Redeemed Hearts
HP583—Ramshackle Rose
HP600—The Restoration
HP624—One Chance in a Million
HP648—Last Chance
HP657—Love Worth Finding
HP688—A Handful of Flowers
HP696—Bridal Veil
HP704—No Buttons or Beaux

Don't miss out on any of our super romances. Write to us at the following address for information on our newest releases and club information.

Heartsong Presents Readers' Service
PO Box 721
Uhrichsville, OH 44683

Or visit www.heartsongpresents.com

Spoke
of Love

Cathy Marie Hake

Heartsong Presents

A note from the Author:
I love to hear from my readers! You may correspond with me by writing:

Cathy Marie Hake
Author Relations
PO Box 721
Uhrichsville, OH 44683

ISBN 1-59310-867-2

SPOKE OF LOVE

All scripture quotations are taken from the King James Version of the Bible.

All of the characters and events in this book are fictitious. Any resemblance to actual persons, living or dead, or to actual events is purely coincidental.

Our mission is to publish and distribute inspirational products offering exceptional value and biblical encouragement to the masses.

PRINTED IN THE U.S.A.

one

Virginia, 1750

Frost silvered the grass of Fredrick Town's common, making it sparkle in the first light of morn. Samuel Walsh stood at the door of the inn and glanced out, knowing he needed to be on his way soon. His breath condensed on the crisp morning air. Pulling his thick wool cloak tighter against the biting chill, he scanned the area. A small movement caught his attention, and he sucked in a surprised breath. There, chained to the hitching post, huddled a woman.

Seeing her set him in motion. No one ought to be treated so cruelly—and especially not a woman. Concern quickened his pulse and lengthened his stride.

The woman formed a tiny ball in a futile attempt to conserve what little warmth she created. She'd tucked her legs under the ragged homespun dress and rested her head betwixt her imprisoned arms. The wind blew, and she failed to even shiver. *Is she alive?*

Samuel pressed his fingers to the side of her cold, cold neck and detected a thready pulse. "God bless you, woman! You're nearly frozen." He whipped off his heavy cape and enveloped her in its warmth. A short chain looped over and around the hitching post, manacling her to the center. As a result, the woman didn't even have enough length to permit her to draw in her arms to conserve her own heat. Sam squatted to serve as a windbreak for her as he reached up to chafe her icy hands.

It took a full minute before the woman dully opened her eyes. They matched the pale gray of an early spring morning mist, and her dazed expression told him she couldn't comprehend why such degradation and suffering were visited upon her.

"There, now," he crooned as he cupped her frigid face between his hands. "You'll be warm soon."

A piteous moan curled in her throat.

Sam looked around. No one else stirred on the common. Metal items cost dearly, but a paltry half-dozen links held her fast. Fresh scrape marks on the wood bespoke her attempts to reach the edge so the chain would fall onto the support piece and allow her to draw in her arms. His hands roared with heat in comparison to hers as he chafed them.

She'd not been here last eve when he arrived. 'Twas already gloaming then, and he'd made haste to see his horse stabled ere he wearily signed the inn's register, partaken of a hot meal, and filled space in the bed he'd hired in the upstairs. Frost on her eyelashes, hair, and shoulders told him she'd suffered out here during the time he'd burrowed under thick blankets.

Resolving to put a stop to this travesty, he squeezed her hands to gain her attention. "Where is your master?"

She opened her mouth, but no words came out. Her head sagged between her arms again.

Samuel briskly rubbed her arms, then cupped her pale cheeks. "I mean to help you."

She stared at him. Tears silvered her eyes, formed rivulets down her grimy cheeks, and disappeared between his fingers. Hopelessness radiated from her.

"I'll be back." Sam rose. "Right back." He stalked toward

the smithy. Surely he'd find an axe there. He'd chop through the hitching post and free the woman in a trice.

"What's this?" A deep voice growled from a distance.

Samuel wheeled around to see a stocky man snatch the cloak from the girl. "Replace that at once!" Samuel ran back.

The pock-faced man booted the woman in the thigh. Even though the action scooted her a good nine inches to the side and stretched her arms to the point that the chain pulled, she barely winced.

"Cease that! There's no cause—"

"She belongs to me." The stranger spat at her feet. "I hold no particular affinity for her, though."

"That's plain enough to see!" Sam reached them and yanked his cloak from the stranger's hands. As he engulfed the girl within the woolen folds again, Sam felt the awful thinness of her shoulders. "Even a beast shouldn't be mistreated so." Samuel gently slid the woman back into place. His glare dared the owner to object. After he'd repositioned her in such a manner that her arms wouldn't be twisted so painfully, Samuel demanded, "Free her and explain yourself."

The man's jaw jutted forward, and he folded his arms across his chest.

"Free her," Samuel snarled. "Now."

Her owner's beady eyes took on a wary cast, and he produced a key. Samuel knew the woman's shoulder and arm muscles would cramp once the heartless owner freed her from the chain. He wasn't sure she could even comprehend much, but he knelt. "I mean no disrespect," he murmured as his hands delved past the sides of her bosom and turned beneath her arms to support the stick-thin limbs as they fell free from the shackles.

Her scrawny muscles twitched and spasmed, yet she compressed her lips and made no sound. Moisture in her eyes tattled on the pain she felt, but she stayed silent. Could it be she was alert enough to realize he'd championed her? *Aye.* A spark of something in her glistening eyes told him 'twas so.

"You'll ne'er be chained again. I vow it." He pulled the cloak tight around her, then rose. Keeping one hand on her shoulder, Samuel glowered. "Explain yourself."

"A ship's captain sold her to me as she slept." The stranger cast a loathsome look at the pitiful woman. "Only five of the dozen brides survived the voyage."

"Twice in the last five years, the store's imported brides. After six weeks at sea, the women could barely walk, let alone wed and work. Couldn't you show her mercy?"

"She deserves none."

"I know not whence you've come," Sam gritted, "but here, slaves and indentured servants normally sleep in the stable, if not on a pallet in the inn."

The stranger merely shrugged.

"Women deserve to be protected and appreciated. If you cannot care gently for her, turn her over to someone who will."

"She's defiant." A sneer twisted the man's features. "I've had her a full fortnight, and she refuses to speak a word. I cannot wed her without her consent, so I've had to take to punishing her until her tongue loosens."

"Poor woman is likely mute!"

"Nay." The man shook his head. "Silence in a woman can be a good thing and in a slave a very good thing, but her silence is not from birth, for she mutters in her sleep. Best she stop this nonsense and learn who's her master."

"So you would leave her to the elements simply because she's been stubborn? This isn't discipline—'tis cruelty!"

"The widow was sold to pay off her husband's debts. I paid good coin for her and won't be cheated."

Sam went back on his knees beside the woman and tightened his cloak about her. "Have you never read the scriptures about caring for the widows and orphans?"

Hands on his hips, the man glowered. "Do you make me an offer?"

Samuel thought of the leather britches he needed. He also recalled how desperately his son Christopher required a shirt. *My family's needs must come first, and someone else will buy the woman. Whoever does, she'll not be much of a bargain. Small, thin, filthy, and mute, she'd make for a pitiful servant. No man would pay a bride price for her—clearly she is far too frail to bear children.*

He looked at the heap of humanity before him and tried to force himself to refuse to part with what little money he had.

She hung her head in a move of abject misery.

She needs my compassion more than she needs my cloak. I promised her my assistance. "I've not much. What do you ask?"

Sam knew full well the scarcity of women. Though neither pretty nor prizes in any other way, the brides in previous shipments didn't step foot inside the store ere men bought them. Indeed, the community gave grieving widows only two or three months of mourning. After that passage of time, the parson approached them about the natural order of living under a man's domination. A marriage usually followed on the very next Sabbath.

Avarice glinted in the stranger's eyes. "Twenty-eight pounds. With only two women for every three men here in the New World, I can get my price. You know I can."

Samuel let out a disbelieving snort. "This one's almost starved and mute!"

"Twenty, then."

Shaking his head, Sam heaved a sigh.

"Eighteen and not a single pence less."

Lord, You know I haven't anywhere near that much. Watch over her and give her to a man who'll treat her with kindness. Regret swamped Samuel as he turned loose of the cloak. The woman slumped sideways. He caught her ere she landed on her side.

The stranger cleared his throat. "Fifteen."

Father of Light, You know I have just over six. What would You have me do? Samuel couldn't let go of her.

"Fifteen pounds," the man repeated.

"A third of that, and you've done better than you ought. She's so weak, no man will offer you more."

"Now see here! Passage alone cost nearly six pounds."

Sam scoffed. "Do you take me for a fool? Six pounds would fund a private cabin. You said there were a dozen brides. Passage for the whole lot of them barely cost six."

Muttering curses, the man tugged the cloak from the girl and yanked her to her feet.

No woman ought ever be subjected to such base language and rough treatment. Samuel made one last attempt to redeem her. " 'Tis abundantly clear her state isn't merely from a difficult voyage. She can't weigh so much as six stone."

Again her owner spat into the dust at her feet. "She's not worth feeding. She rendered no service to me."

Samuel stepped between them to protect her from the other man's crudity. Anger vibrated in his voice. "If she dies—and from the looks of her, that could well happen—those men you said would pay so dearly for her will convict you of murder."

Sam sensed her collapsing behind him, but he didn't move.

Fear flashed in the stranger's eyes. "Five pounds—in coin only. No paper money."

Elation filled him, but Sam kept his expression chilly. "The only papers will be hers, and you'll yield them to me at once."

"They're inside."

Samuel grabbed his cloak from the dirt and shook it. "Go fetch the papers." He knelt in the dirt by the woman and tucked his cloak about her yet again. "Just a little while longer. I'll have you away from him. Just awhile longer." Sure the owner was out of sight, Samuel yanked off a boot. Two toes poked out of a hole in his stocking. Perhaps the woman would be able to darn it, but from the looks of her, not for a moon or longer. Coins spilled into his hand, and Sam counted out five pounds, then hastily dumped the remainder into his boot and tugged it back on.

No more had he gotten to his feet when the man returned. "Her papers. Give me the money."

Samuel inspected the papers. Finding all in order, he yielded the hard-earned money and turned back to the woman. He softly called her by the name on her papers. "Garnet Wheelock?"

Her eyes opened.

Samuel gave her what he hoped was a reassuring smile and brought the woman to her feet. Her legs threatened to buckle, but she caught the hitching post and stayed upright. No doubt, sheer dint of will was all that kept her on her feet. He wound an arm about her waist to lend her support and warmth, then bade, "Come."

Her head wobbled in what he took as nod of agreement,

and she put one foot in front of the other. Her gait seemed oddly stilted. Sam quickly deduced she locked her knees with each step so her legs wouldn't give out. He felt the iron resolve beneath the shivering of her reedlike body. "I'll lift you. Your limbs cannot serve to step o'er the doorsill."

It took nothing at all to sweep her into his arms, and Samuel knew a moment's remorse for having given over such valuable coin for her. She would be too small and weak to serve at hard tasks. She must have sensed his hesitance, because the girl slid a hand out of the cloak and clenched his doublet in desperation.

"Rest your fear. I'd not give you back to such a fiend." He strode back to the inn and headed straight for the hearth. Once there, he settled her into a rough-hewn pine chair. "Stay here to gather warmth, and I'll fetch food for you."

"Eh!" The serving wench flapped her arms like a farmwife trying to shoo a pesky murder of crows from her newly sown field. "Get that baggage out!"

Placing a hand on his "baggage's" thin shoulder, Samuel steadied her ere she tumbled over. "The woman will partake of the meal intended for me. Have mercy on her."

"Mercy? Only the Almighty can do that! This is a proper place. We allow none of her ilk."

"The poor woman is near frozen and in need of sustenance. I'll not permit any to gainsay me." He gave the wench a piercing stare. "I've not asked more than my share. Since I've allotted my portion to her, you've no cause to object. Bring the food."

The serving wench's nose assumed a defiant tilt.

Samuel drew up a three-legged stool directly in front of the frail woman, eased his weight onto it, and gently tucked a tangle of hair behind her shoulder. He'd never seen such a filthy woman; but 'twas not her doing, and he couldn't fault her. On the other hand, he did hold the serving wench to blame for her cold manner. He turned and gave her the same stern look he used for his children when they balked at doing a chore.

Lips pursed as though she'd tasted something sour, the wench flounced to a scarred pine sideboard and ladled a modest portion of the barley-and-oat gruel into a chipped pottery bowl. She cast a sly look at him.

Unwilling to let her goad him, he pasted on a smile. "You have my thanks, mistress, for adding both butter and cream to that."

Once he accepted the bowl, Samuel stirred it. He took a small bite to test the temperature. Satisfied, he lifted a generous spoonful of gruel to his charge's mouth and quietly urged her to eat. She obediently swallowed, but she wasn't able to take in much. When it became apparent she'd eat no more, Samuel finished off the bowl and set it aside.

"Do you thirst, little one?" The small flicker of her smile was answer enough. Choosing not to trouble the serving wench again, Samuel rose and paced to the sideboard. Pewter pitchers of milk and ale rested there. He poured a tankard of the former and carried it back to the little scrap of a woman he'd purchased. She remained huddled within the thick folds of his cloak. She needed to warm up, and as he'd deemed her too weak to hold the beverage, Samuel resumed his seat on the stool and tilted the tankard to her cracked lips. Sip after sip she took—small ones, but they added up until she managed to drink half of the milk. She then looked at him, lifted her chin, and seemed to silently urge him to finish the rest.

"You may have it all. There's plenty."

She shook her head. It was more a weak wobble than anything, but since she communicated her refusal clearly, he drained the remainder of the creamy milk, then twisted to the side and set the tankard on a sticky tabletop.

He turned back to her and gently rested his palm on her thigh. She cringed at his touch, and her face twisted in embarrassed dismay. "Calm your heart, woman," Samuel rumbled softly as he gently rubbed his thumb back and forth a discreet inch. "I merely wish to inquire whether his kick did you any damage."

She shook her head.

"Very well." Samuel rose. He had no goods with him, so he simply lifted her into his arms. "Because I've matters to attend, you'll need to pass a bit of time."

Her lips parted slightly as her brows knit.

"Don't be troubled. I vow I'll come back for you." The way she shivered cut him to the core. Was it from fear or from cold? Most likely both, and that vexed him. She deserved every shred of reassurance and comfort he could give. He stepped over the threshold and murmured, "Since the woman here displays neither mercy nor charity, I'll bear you off to the stable. It can shelter you until I return."

The woman blinked.

"I count it a pity that wench showed you no understanding. Forgive her, if you can. 'Tis a small heart she must have, and that will make for a miserable life."

He snuggled the mute closer and injected a bit of merriment in his voice to ease the dread in her eyes. "As for you—I suppose you could ponder upon the fact that sleeping in a stable is a blessed thing to do. Our Lord spent His very first nights in one."

She let out a sigh and rested her temple lightly in the crook of his neck.

The stable lay a stone's throw away from the inn. The stalls boasted generous heaps of fresh straw. Any of the servants or slaves who slept here last night had arisen and started their duties. Satisfied she'd be alone and safe, Samuel easily carried his burden to the farthest stall. Once he reached it, he shook his head. His horse had been watered, well fed, and warm for the night; the woman in his arms hadn't received even a fraction of that basic attention.

He nudged his mare to the side. The stall still held a fair layer of straw, which Sam kicked into a small heap. He knelt before it. For a moment, the position brought to mind all the times he had knelt at the fireside and gathered his sons for a bedtime prayer. Odd that such a thought should flash through his mind, yet he felt the presence of the Lord in that warm, quiet moment.

"Rest here." He laid the woman in the straw. "I must get supplies, and then I'll take you home with me. I fear I left my blanket in the wagon over at the miller's. The straw may itch, but it'll keep you warmer. Pray, forgive me." He tucked his cloak around her more closely before he took an armful of straw from the adjacent stall and piled it over her thin body. He made sure her face stayed clear, but the achingly sad beauty of her eyes took him aback. He gave her a tender smile and whispered roughly, "Rest."

❧

At first, Garnet Wheelock thought this was a tall, broadly built man who possessed an exceedingly kind heart; but now, she knew different. With the morning sun shining through the open stable doors far behind him, a strange, golden nimbus radiated around the edge of his dark brown hair. Golden shards brightened the centers of his deep brown eyes.

He must be an angel—the angel of death. *I never knew death would wrap me in warmth and whisper kind words. Lord, I'm ready. I come not on my own merit, but because the Lamb's blood covered my sins.*

"Rest," the angel bade her.

This moment of security was probably the euphoria of a dying mind, but she sank into that comfort and thanked heaven for the mercy of being given a peaceful dream in her final moments. Heaven was but a breath away.

"I'll soon take you away from here."

Everything rippled as if a pool of blissfully warm water were closing around her. As she started to drift off, her last sight was of the angel's compassionate smile. Soon the terrible memories would be purged from her mind.

two

Samuel knelt by the woman and watched as exhaustion claimed her. Plainly, the flame of life within her barely flickered anymore. Filth streaked her face and clothes, and she was gaunt with near starvation. He'd seen the depth of emotion shimmering in her eyes, though—and he knew that deep within the woman possessed a soul worth fostering.

Deciding he'd done the right thing, Samuel rose, led his horse to the stable yard, and mounted. At the miller's, he reclaimed his cornmeal, rye, and wheat flour. The miller withheld the customary sixth of the grain as his payment, and Samuel helped him load the balance in large barrels onto the wagon.

" 'Twas excellent corn," the miller praised. "Fine flavor. My woman made hasty pudding with it last eve."

" 'Tis a blessing to have a goodwife who cares sweetly for you."

"Aye." The miller curled his flour-dusted hand around a wagon wheel. "Your milling bore a third of one more barrel. I'm willing to trade for more of it. Would you accept maple syrup?"

"I've syrup aplenty."

"I've cider—sweet and smooth. Perchance a basket of apples and three jugs of cider?"

Samuel looked at the barrels of cornmeal, then back at the miller. He didn't want to make an enemy, but the deal seemed less than fair. "A basket of apples?"

A sheepish smile tilted the miller's lips. "Make it three baskets of apples and four jugs of cider."

"Done."

When the miller's apprentice brought out the first basket of apples, Samuel's eyes widened. "I mistook your barter for a bushel! I feel it unfair to take three baskets now. 'Tis not an even barter."

The miller chuckled. "Yonder is my orchard—look at how fruitful it is this year. I'll truthfully not miss the apples at all. Your willingness to reconsider the barter to my advantage pleases me. Take all three in good health as a blessing to your house."

"You have my heartiest thanks." Samuel actually needed help hefting the crate-sized baskets up onto the wagon. The miller's apprentice grunted as they finished the last one.

Samuel cleared his throat. He didn't want to have to pay for the beautiful, large baskets. "I'll return these containers when next I—"

The miller let out a boisterous laugh. "Don't bother. An old man and his lackwit son live in the woods beyond the edge of town. They weave these baskets and barter for flour and meal with them. I've more baskets than sense, and I'd rather have you come back to me for milling than to go elsewhere. I'll consider it an investment in hopes of getting more of your corn next season."

"Be assured, I'll return. I venture God will reward you for this kindness. I and they are blessed by your generosity." He shook the miller's hand and drove off in a well-stocked wagon.

Samuel took the grain to the mercantile. With no wife at home, he'd been forced to barter or pay for simple items. It rankled him to have to rely on his wife's sister to keep his sweet little daughter, Hester. Naomi had been a shrewish wife to him, and her sister, Dorcas, held the same temperament. If the woman he had just bought turned out to be half as stubborn or foul natured, he'd have her gone in a trice.

Lord, 'tis badly done of me to think such dark thoughts about her. I've prayed You'd make a way for me to bring home my beloved Hester. If this woman I've bought is of godly persuasion and sweet spirit, she'll prove to be a blessing. I've no wish to marry again. Since she's been sold off to pay for her husband's debts, she's likely soured on the notion of marriage, too.

"Ho, now," the shopkeeper said as he approached. "What can I sell you today?"

"I've grain to barter," Samuel started out. "I require molasses, an ax head, and powder for my flintlock."

"I presume you'll also want metal for molding bullets."

Sam shook his head. "I've enough at home, but you can show me a shirt length of cloth, a needle, and thread."

"Cloth and metal are expensive," the shopkeeper warned. "Especially since the Crown passed the Iron Act, cost has gone up considerably. What grain did you bring, and how much do you have to trade?"

His harvest rendered a slightly larger yield than Sam expected, but he hesitated to part with much. Adding little Hester and the woman to his family meant more mouths to feed. Bartering away much of the surplus would be foolish. "I'd need to know your prices before I can estimate what I'll spare you."

"They're posted on the counter." The shopkeeper wandered toward a woman who stood by a small shelf before a display of spices. "Cloves. Fragrant, aren't they?"

Sam reviewed the prices and winced. He desperately needed leather britches. Woven ones wore out too fast, and he couldn't afford to buy more cloth—even if the woman he'd bought this morning sewed for him and spared his family the expense of hiring a tailor. A leather pair would last indefinitely, but after spending so much on the waif, Samuel knew he'd have to make do with what he currently owned.

Any misgivings he felt in the store disappeared when he returned to the stable. "Ma'am," he said softly. The woman didn't respond to him, so he gently pushed away the straw. A wayward strand of hair fluttered in the shallow currents of her silent breaths. Though he addressed her again, the woman didn't rouse in the least. Sam slid his arms beneath her and lifted.

Never had he seen an exhaustion so profound, yet surprise rippled through him when the move didn't cause her to stir or make her breathing hitch. Carefully, he placed her in the back of his wagon in the spot he'd left free to accommodate her.

When the sun almost reached its zenith and they had traversed a quarter of the way to his homestead, the wagon hit a rut deep enough to jar it badly. She woke with a gasp and bolted upright.

≈

"All is well; all is well," a deep voice murmured.

For a few moments, Garnet felt disoriented. She couldn't recall where she was or whom she was with. Shoving back her snarled hair, she saw her angel of death. It took a moment to realize he wasn't a heavenly being but a mortal man. Memories of his kindness that morning surfaced. *Lord, if 'tisn't my time to be borne to Your bosom, You have my thanks for letting me belong to a compassionate man.*

"How do you fare?"

His inquiry jarred her out of her musings. Though embarrassed, she timidly looked off to the side of the road and hoped he'd guess at her quandary.

"You've slept a good while. I suppose you'd like a moment to yourself. We'll stop yonder. There's a small stream there."

Garnet nodded and folded her hands in her lap. When the wagon stopped, the man wrapped the reins about the brake, jumped down in a single, lithe move, and reached up for her. "Here, now."

I'd rather scramble down unassisted, but that might offend him.

A winsome smile tugged at the corner of his mouth. "I didn't judge well. There's a mud puddle over on the other side."

His admission disarmed her. Garnet half stood, and he cupped her waist. It took every scrap of her self-control not to flinch. Her fingers fleetingly made contact with his broad shoulders as he lifted her down.

Instead of immediately letting go, he braced her waist. Fire streaked from his fingers clear up her back, but she tamped down her urge to twist free.

"I see slumber restored a bit of your strength."

She nodded.

"Do you need me to carry you behind the bushes?"

She emphatically refused by shaking her head.

He finally turned loose and cleared his throat. "Then go and be assured of your privacy. I vow I'll give you your due. Take your time and fear not."

She twitched what she hoped would pass for a smile and went off behind a bush. A wary glance over her shoulder confirmed the man kept his word. He stood with his back to her, so she gratefully ventured to the edge of the stream.

Shoving up dirt-encrusted sleeves, she knelt on the bank.

Her reflection left her gasping. Snarls, oil, and dirt abounded in her tresses. She'd been able to see how grimy her hands had grown, but her face was even worse. Rivulets streaked her cheeks from when she'd wept this morning. Her new master must possess infinite kindness for yielding over so much money for her. She couldn't remedy her hair at the moment, but at least she could wash the worst off her flesh.

Sand from the bank bit into her palm. *Sand, Lord. You've provided sand so I can scour away the filth.* Face, arms, hands, and even the back of her neck—the cool water and abrasive sand scrubbed them clean. Another glance let her know her master continued to face away, so she even furtively lifted her skirt and whisked dampened hands over her legs.

When she returned, the stranger reached out and took her hands. A smile creased his kind face. "Being slovenly clearly isn't your way. The papers give your name as Garnet Wheelock, but that is all. I've no notion what to expect of a woman bearing such a fanciful name."

How can I make this man understand I'll work hard for him? Garnet went down on her knees and placed his hand on her head.

"I'll have none of that. No one ought kneel to another. Such obeisance is reserved only for the good Lord."

Garnet rose.

He nodded his approval. "I am Samuel Walsh, a planter by trade. In the days ahead, we'll come to learn more about one another. For now, I'm eager to be on the way. My sons are staying at the Mortons'." He frowned as she tried to dust off her skirts. "First, we'll go by Goodwife Stamsfield's. Perchance she has a bit of soap we can buy."

Garnet thought for a moment, then wrung her hands.

"You're nervous?"

The pantomime hadn't transmitted her meaning. She tried again, rubbing her palms together, and then holding them side by side and blowing on them. She then formed a circle with her thumb and forefinger to depict a soap bubble rising.

"Soap!"

Her head bobbed, and she tapped her breastbone to transmit that she'd make it for him.

Samuel Walsh grinned. "Ah, so you can make soap. I'll ask you to do that soon. I've little left at home."

She bobbed her head in assent. Mayhap things would turn out passably well.

three

Garnet Wheelock wasn't a brazen woman. Indeed, she acted as bashfully as any modest woman might. Samuel kept a mental catalog of her traits. Since he knew nothing about her, he had good cause to wonder about her character. To this point, she had exhibited the virtues of modesty and cleanliness. He'd not yet seen a vice, but those might remain hidden for a short while ere she became comfortable and let down her guard.

After assessing the length of the shadows on the ground, he proclaimed, "We're making good time home. Let's continue." He lifted her into the wagon. Pain flickered across her features. "Are you ailing?"

She averted her eyes and shook her head.

After climbing up, he turned her back to face him. His hand cupped her jaw. "I'm not a man to value deception."

Her slender fingers shook as she haltingly reached up and gingerly wrapped them around his wrist. She hadn't the strength to remove his hand, but it was clear from the way she stiffened and shied away that she was not one to welcome a stranger's touch, however innocent it might be.

"As you wish." He sighed, then turned back, grabbed his cloak, and swirled it about her. "At least keep warm. I'll have Goodwife Morton see to you."

She clutched the cloak around herself and let out a soundless sigh. The wagon set into motion. They continued on in a strange but companionable silence. At one point, Garnet patted his arm and pointed ahead a short distance.

"Grapes, eh?"

She nodded and hopped off the wagon. Heavily laden, the conveyance trundled slowly enough to allow her to scamper ahead. A timid smile creased her face as Samuel drew close. Having identified wild grapes, she gathered a handful and raised them to him. Sweeping her hand back toward the vines, she arched a brow.

"Whoa!" The wagon halted, and he looked behind him in the wagon for something to hold the unexpected bounty. Nodding to himself, he stepped into the bed and rummaged. "I bought cloth. . . . Here it is. By knotting it, I might be able to empty most of the apples from one basket into it. Then we can fill that basket with grapes."

She shook her head and gestured.

"No?"

Garnet pointed at each of the baskets, then held her hands apart.

"There's a fine plan. I'll remove some apples from each basket and knot them into the cloth; then we can pile grapes on the top of the baskets."

Garnet beamed and nodded.

The stop took very little time, but Sam considered the yield more than worth the moments spent. When the baskets were full, Garnet harvested one last bunch. Samuel got the water jug he kept under the wagon seat and rinsed them. They shared the unexpected bounty as their nuncheon.

Samuel lifted Garnet back into the wagon and got underway. Juice stained his fingers, and he noted her hands and lips were tinted, too. She looked a bit better all washed up and rested. "I confess," he stated as he leaned toward her a little, "I'm experiencing the sin of pride. I'm returning home with a woman to help my children, apples, and grapes that were all unexpected."

She folded her stained hands together as if in prayer, then pressed her lips to them and opened them. She lifted her palms heavenward, as if in thanksgiving.

"Aye, we give thanks to God for His generosity."

When the sun hung low in the sky, he pulled to a small bend in the road. "We'll need to stop here to pass the night." She seemed to understand, but he wasn't sure what kind of life she formerly led. A country girl would have full understanding of what an evening stop entailed; a city-born one—either slave or servant—would be completely ignorant of the necessary tasks. This stop would reveal a fair bit about her. "There's a creek just behind that stand of trees. I'll water the horse."

She nodded and let him help her down. As he unhitched, she looked around and gathered up some twigs and a few pieces of wood.

Samuel watered the horse, returned, and nodded approvingly at the well-constructed formation of tinder and small pieces of wood in the center of the stone circle she'd created. He felt a small flare of relief. She might well serve his family in acceptable fashion by at least doing mild tasks about the homestead. "Well done, Mistress Wheelock. I've flint in the wagon under the seat."

She hastened to the wagon for the desired flint and soon had a small fire going. Once it caught, she went off for a necessary moment. On the way back, she gathered more wood.

"You're not a sluggardly woman, I must say." He handed

her an apple after she released her hold on the wood and allowed it to tumble to the ground.

She smiled her thanks for both the apple and the praise, bowed her head in thanks, then jerked away when his hand covered hers.

Samuel looked at her somberly. Her eyes were huge, and her lips began to quiver. *I scared her.* He made a note to be more cautious with his contact. Using the low, lazy tone he employed when soothing his children from their nightmares, he said, "You can count me as a friend. I merely wished to voice the blessing, seeing as yours is one I cannot hear to share." He gave a simple, heartfelt prayer, then let go of her. He skewered a sausage on a green stick, and she silently took it from him.

She was such an enigma. Filthy, but clean-handed. Gentle, yet strangely remote. In spite of her ragged clothing, she showed an odd dignity. She knelt gracefully by the fire, nudged a small log so it would burn more evenly, and cooked the sausage. Instead of holding the stick over the flames, she skillfully propped the end of it between two heavy stones so the sausage arced over the fire and roasted.

Samuel made no pretense about watching her. He needed to take her measure. A city girl might have enough common sense to take care of a fire, but she'd not know to prop a cooking stick in this fashion. She'd have chosen a dry, brittle stick instead of a supple, green one, too. She wouldn't have identified the grapes at such a distance, either. Garnet showed more promise as the day passed. What she lacked in strength, she made up for with knowledge.

Samuel watched as Garnet checked the sausage once more. She seemed satisfied that it was beginning to sizzle its way to perfection. That done, she took a pair of apples from the wagon. After wrapping the fruit in a few large leaves, she carefully put it in the ashes to cook.

"There's a good idea. It'll be a sweet treat, and one to warm you a mite."

She turned the sausage. It put off a savory aroma, and the way it sizzled made his mouth water. A handful of minutes passed ere the sky went dark. The warmth and light of the fire were welcome against the eerie black of the night.

Samuel sliced the sausage in half and handed her one. Garnet tore her portion in half yet again and gave him the other piece. Her smile faltered as she kept only a quarter of the offering.

"Aren't you hungry, little one?"

She lifted her piece of sausage and the apple, as if to say, "This is enough."

He sighed. "I suppose it is sufficient for someone so small and depleted." The leery look on her face spoke volumes. He quickly tacked on, "Garnet, I do not anticipate hunger this winter. God has been gracious, and in time, you will gain enough from His bounty to fill out into a healthy form. I've no plans to cast you off in your frailty."

Tears of gratitude sparkled in her eyes.

"Sit and eat," he bade.

Garnet waited until he scissored his legs and folded down into a comfortable spot; then she sat a good yard away. Samuel said nothing about the distance she put betwixt them. When she finished eating, she got up and rubbed sand, then tall grass between her hands to clean them. Although the stream wasn't far off, it had grown too dark to wander away from the fire.

Using a knot he pried from one of the pieces of firewood, Samuel put it on a thin, flat rock and set it afire. Garnet looked intently at the odd arrangement.

" 'Tis a knot lamp." He tilted his hand so she could see it more easily. "I presume you've never seen one afore, but all about us is a bounty God provided to meet our needs. This will last a fair while and provide enough light to take care of essential trips. I'll step away a moment. When I return, you might well use it for your privacy, too. I'll not want you to rise in the night. There is safety only by a fire."

She acknowledged his words, and he left. When he returned, Garnet accepted the knot lamp and left the immediate area. She attended to her needs and swiftly returned to their tiny camp.

The small knot lamp illuminated her features softly, and Samuel wondered if beneath all of the grime she might actually be pretty. He sternly reminded himself that appearance was a worldly matter, and one that didn't bear much thought. The quality of her character needed to be determined, for that was where a person's true beauty lay. He'd learned that bitter lesson soon after he'd wed.

As he put a few more pieces of wood on the fire and watched them catch, Sam stated in an even voice, "I've but my cloak and a single blanket, Garnet. The night will be bitterly cold. We had frost this morn, and from the look of the moon, we'll have a thicker one again tonight. I vow I'll not abuse you, but I plan for us to share those coverings."

Garnet gave him a wary look and ventured to shake her head tensely. She knelt by the fire and patted the ground there, as if to let him know the fire's warmth would be enough for her.

Ignoring her, Samuel took the blanket over to a shallow indentation in the ground he'd filled with leaves and pine needles. He spread the blanket over them, wishing he could offer her something warmer, more comfortable, and all her own. When he looked up, she glanced over at the wagon and pointed. Then she folded her hands and lay her cheek on them.

"Nay, Garnet. I'll not have you sleep beneath the wagon. Though that would normally be the best way for us to stay warm, you've coughed a bit already today. The flour and cornmeal put off a fine dust, and 'twould sift down on you. I've gathered more wood—that fact should bear witness of my certitude we'll have a cold night."

She stared at the pile of wood he'd supplied. The corners of her mouth drooped.

Sam walked to her and held out his hand. "Come, Garnet. I've given you my word. You've nothing to fear from me. I'm an honorable man. I'll give you my back this night."

Even by firelight, he could see how her face flamed. He felt ungallant for this insistence, knowing full well this turn of events appalled her. Still, the temperature had already begun to drop. She was piteously thin and had barely survived the previous night. If she weren't kept warm, little Garnet wouldn't make it through another cold night without taking ill.

A small whimper trembled deep in her throat, and her eyes stayed huge. Garnet bowed her head.

"Come, then." He stooped, lifted her, and carried her to the blanket. She seemed so frail in his arms. She probably didn't weigh any more than his ten-year-old son. Samuel paused for a moment and gently swayed her from side to side in a small arc, much as he had his children when they were babes and in want of soothing. The way she'd gone so tense in his arms and stopped breathing cut him to the heart. *God, bless this woman.*

Only You know what she's endured.

He laid her down to face the fire, then took the knife from his sheath. She jolted upright as a strangled sound of fear curled in her throat. Samuel restrained her with one hand while he flipped up the edge of the blanket and laid the knife beneath. That hand came up to cup her gaunt cheek. "I gave you my knife for the night. I hope having that at hand gives you reassurance."

If anything, her shoulders curled inwardly even more.

Samuel carefully checked his flintlock, and she watched his every move. He observed her out of the corner of his eye. As he set another smallish branch to the fire, the widow lay down. Aye, she did, and he noted how her fingers located the knife beneath the blanket. Not that he blamed her. Sam took his place beside her, then pulled the cloak up to cover them both. The leaves crackled and rustled beneath them. His back pressed against hers, but she immediately shifted a few inches away.

"Sleep, Garnet. Your fears are groundless." He made an effort to breathe slowly and evenly. It might make her believe he was falling asleep. In truth, he didn't feel overly tired. He knew she must be, though. Clearly, the rest she'd gotten today was insufficient. The deep shadows beneath her eyes bore mute testimony to that fact.

Radiating warmth from the fire teamed with the heat he created. Her weakened state and a full belly conspired against her. Samuel knew from the way she shifted and shook her head that Garnet tried to battle the fatigue, but it eventually overcame her defenses. Finally, she went still and slack. At least she'd found refuge in sleep. He whispered a word of thanksgiving for that small favor. Rest would restore her.

&

She wept in her sleep.

Her thin shoulders heaved with the harsh sobs. Samuel rolled over and tucked the cloak around Garnet more closely and studied her. He wasn't sure of her age. According to her papers, she was a widow. Since she'd been sold to cover her husband's debts, he must have died quite recently. Young and fragile as she seemed, he'd addressed her as Mistress Wheelock all day. Standard convention would change that to Widow Wheelock. Samuel determined to give her the choice of which address they'd use. Fresh grief might well be causing her to weep now, and calling her widow would twist the knife of cruelty into her.

Jumbled sounds came from her mouth, mixing with her heartrending sobs. Her mouth was lush, but a scab darkened her lower lip. Clearly, her owner had struck her. He'd kicked her, too. *And she was terrified when I explained how we'd have to spend the night.* Sickened to the depths of his soul at how she must have suffered, Sam watched the firelight flicker across her delicate features. *Lord, You alone know everything this poor little woman's suffered. Even when her body has long since healed, her heart will ache. Be merciful to her. You've placed her in my keeping. Allow her to find safety and peace.*

Sam quelled the almost overwhelming urge to smooth her tangled hair and soothe her. He'd given his word he'd give her his back. If she woke to his touch, she'd panic. Instead, he carefully leaned over Garnet and forcefully shoved another log on the fire. Unable to break his word and hold her, he very gently murmured, "Garnet, come now. Roll over." To his relief, she obligingly turned over.

"Good, good," he whispered as he took her far hand in

his. Samuel lay down again and gave Garnet his back once more, but he shifted back and tugged her palm so she half squirmed until her chest and cheek were pressed to his spine. A choppy sigh exited her, and she seemed to calm—at least he hoped she'd calmed. To his relief, she no longer shuddered with those oh-so-quiet, body-wracking sobs that tugged at his heart and soul. He lay there and clasped her small hand in his.

She was nothing more than a hank of tangled hair and a few thin bones—and a gentle smile and possessed of a tender spirit. His feelings took him by surprise. He tamped them down. The woman needed brotherly love. She'd tried to clean up, but in truth, she still stank. He smiled wryly as he let that realization dampen the attraction he felt. A short while later, he drifted off to sleep with her cuddled up behind him.

Samuel woke before she did. He carefully slithered a few inches from her and quietly rose. She lay burrowed in his cloak, her face obscured by its folds and her snarled hair. He tucked the edges of the blanket back over her. She'd shivered the whole night long, and he'd struggled to keep his vow. Had he been able to envelop her in his arms, he'd undoubtedly have warmed the wraithlike woman far better. Her conduct from the start kept him more than aware of her opinion of men, though, and he couldn't very well expect her to hold him in any esteem if he proved to be a liar.

The way she cringed from even the simplest touch and cried in the night troubled him. What harm had come to her in captivity? There was no way for her to tell him, though he couldn't help being curious. Then again, it was none of his business, and to bring those memories up might be too much for her.

His neighbor's wife might be of some help. Ruth Morton had a quiet way about her that made it easy for others to divulge confidences and troubles. Mayhap keeping company with a woman would bring Garnet some peace of heart.

Just before daybreak, he'd added the last bit of wood to the fire and silently prayed she'd at least not suffer any untoward effects from the biting chill. She'd be safe enough now. Samuel stalked off. After visiting the creek and watering the horse, he knelt and reluctantly shook Mistress Wheelock's shoulder.

She bolted up and scrambled back away from him in a reflexive move.

four

"Good morrow." Master Walsh studied her. After a long moment, he gave her the slightest smile and gestured at a small pot at the edge of the fire. "I've made corn mush. There's but one spoon. Go on to the creek to splash yourself awake and break your fast. We must journey onward."

The pounding of her heart slowed. Garnet nodded. After eating, she took great care to make sure to extinguish all the embers. The task left her feeling warm and sticky.

"Well done." Master Walsh nodded toward the fire ring. "One spark, and the whole area would be aflame. I'm done hitching Butterfly to the wagon, so let's get on the way."

Garnet gave him a quizzical look and mouthed, "Butterfly?"

A pleasant chuckle bubbled out of him. "My daughter named the mare. 'Twas the most beautiful thing she could think of, thus the name. I humored her."

Affection rang in his tone, and Garnet couldn't help smiling. Yesterday, he'd said they'd stop and pick up his sons. He'd not spoken of his daughter. Neither had he mentioned a wife. Her smile faded. *If only he would tell me more of his family.*

"Come, we must move on." He beckoned her. As soon as she reached his side, her master reached for his cloak. "The morning air still holds a chill. Here."

Garnet stepped back and patted the blanket.

"No, no." He shook his head. "I'm plenty warm enough. You're a tiny bird of a woman. Let this warm you." He enveloped her in the folds of his cloak.

She cringed.

His eyes darkened, and the gold centers dimmed. His face went somber, as did his tone. "You need never fear me."

Unable to respond with words, she twitched him an apologetic smile.

" 'Twas an explanation, not a chide," he said softly as he cupped his hands about her waist. "Now up you go."

Garnet scooted to the far side of the bench. Once they set out, she couldn't decide what to do. The cloak made her too hot, but when she shrugged out of it, she started to shiver.

"Put it across your lap, girl." His voice stayed low and gentle. "We've half the day's travel. Soon you'll see an open meadow. Game likes to graze there, and I make it a habit to keep my flintlock loaded."

She nodded. Only a fool left his firearm unloaded. Garnet looked at his flintlock and knew a raw twist of memory. Her husband had owned one. She knew how to clean and load it. In truth, hunger once drove her to fire it. The bruise on her shoulder lasted three weeks and served as a remembrance of that fruitless effort.

Garnet never fired it again—not because she feared the inevitable pain in her shoulder but because Cecil wagered and lost the flintlock. It was yet another vital thing he'd sacrificed due to his gambling. In the seven months of their marriage, they'd work their small farm by day. By night, Cecil had squandered anything their labor achieved—hay, ham, milk, a bushel of peas, the pewter dishes from their table, and even the blankets from their bed. Item after item disappeared from their humble home—each toted away by someone who bested her husband at cards.

She wondered about Samuel Walsh. He hadn't said, "A woman to help my wife" or "A woman to help my family." Was he a widower? He'd mentioned a daughter and sons—how many did he have? How old were they? He provided well for them. Then, too, he was a man who showed generosity and compassion—and restraint. He'd not touched her in an untoward manner. Garnet shuddered.

He shot her a questioning look. She dipped her head and fussed with the cloak, pleating its folds over her lap.

"Your silence gives a man ample room to exercise his patience and control his curiosity."

Garnet peeped out of the corner of her eye. Was he mad? No, his lips were tilted in a grin. She let out a relieved sigh and rested her hands beneath the thick woolen cloth. Quiet descended between them. Birds' songs, the wind soughing through the trees, and the mare's steady *clop-clop-clop* filled the crisp air. Her previous owner spent most of the time berating and punishing her. This man's silence carried no bitterness or anger, and the lines radiating from the corners of his eyes hinted that he laughed often and easily.

Almighty God, have You brought me halfway around the world and now blessed me with safety? Please, Lord, let it be so.

Weariness dragged at her. Garnet wakened, horrified to discover she'd slumped against her new master's side. Her face rested against his sleeve. It smelled of smoke, pine, and lye soap. She gasped and sat upright at once.

"You barely rested at all," he stated mildly. He was kind enough to omit mentioning how she'd made use of his arm for a pillow. "I'd suppose you're in need of much rest yet. Did you have a rough voyage?"

She nodded grimly and stared bleakly off to the side. He

seemed to respect her wish to reveal nothing more, and for that she was grateful. The wagon wheels hit a rut and cracked loudly. The sound alarmed an enormous bird that hid in tall grasses not far off.

The flintlock boomed loudly next to her, making her jump.

"Bless us! We'll have fowl this night!" He put down the firearm and jerked back on the reins at the same time. Once the horse halted, her master was off to get the fowl he'd downed. He held the bird by the legs and strode back to the wagon.

Resting the stock of his flintlock on the floor of the wagon, Garnet clamped the long barrel between her knees. It measured four feet long, so she needed to rise up on tiptoe to pour a spoonful of powder into the muzzle. She made a patch with a small bit of buckskin and a ball from the bullet pouch, then tamped it down with the rod. She carefully put her master's firearm back in the exact same location and the very same angle as it had been as they rode.

"No doubt you've seen a turkey before, but they're wild and for the taking here. Back in England, the sumptuary laws make them cost dearly; in the colonies, instead of having them just for Christmas, we dine on them whenever God blesses us." He put the turkey at the back of the wagon. "I have a friend who keeps a flock on his farm. He clips their wings, so they can't fly, then drives them through his tobacco fields. They're good at eating worms off his plants."

She looked at the tom. Her hands came up and flew wide to indicate that she thought him to be of notable size.

"Aye, this fellow will make a few fine meals."

Sam had already slit the neck to bleed the turkey. Garnet crawled to the back and hauled the bird onto her lap. She pulled out the first few large feathers and set them aside.

Looking up at him, she held one up in a silent query.

"Save the largest, but let the rest go. We've nothing to save them in, and a turkey left unplucked ends up having to be skinned to rid it of the feathers. The meat becomes all dry and charred in that eventuality."

She bobbed her head in acknowledgment and set to work at once as he went to get the flintlock. Inspecting his weapon carefully, her master came back and lifted it up a few inches. "How much powder did you put in?"

Too much powder would make it explode. Too little would be a waste. It was a reasonable question. She made him understand just how much and what steps she'd taken.

" 'Twas done as I would have. I've not seen a woman load a firearm ere this, and you did so correctly. Did you do it because I said I always kept her loaded?"

She nodded.

"And you've done the task ofttimes afore, haven't you?"

She bit her lip and nodded again.

"Garnet, I'm not upset with you. I'm near poleaxed, though. I've had a mother and a wife, and neither ever loaded a weapon. It never occurred to me that a woman might have gained that useful skill. Tell me this, though: If you load her again, how am I to know the deed is done?"

Garnet didn't even have to think. Setting the turkey aside, she took the flintlock from him, plucked out a single strand of her hair, and wound it three times around the trigger guard. Handing the flintlock back, she calmly resumed her work on the turkey.

"We will keep that as our signal. Aye, we will. 'Tis both clever and easy. As I grab the weapon, I'll know at once by feel without having to take my eyes from the target."

She nodded.

Samuel stooped and inspected the wagon. "I was hoping I didn't crack the wheel on that rut. The noise flushed out our supper, but I fretted that it boded ill for the wagon. 'Twasn't anything more than a dry stick in the bottom of the rut."

They went on, and Garnet quickly plucked the huge bird. By poking the largest feathers between fruit, she preserved enough to use as basting brushes. Being in the wagon's bed lent her an opportunity to take stock of the contents. Yesternoon, her master mentioned apples and grapes. Those counted as a small portion of what he hauled.

Spotty school attendance lent her enough skill to read simple words. Barrels bore chalked words. Garnet tilted her head and read. *Rye. Flour.* The next word was the longest. She studied it and felt a flare of happiness. *Cornmeal.* Cornmeal from the Colonies cost dearly in England, and the few occasions when she'd eaten bread or mush from that grain left Garnet with a taste for more. She counted two barrels each of the rye and flour, eight of cornmeal. They must not eat wheat bread as much here.

The apples—what a boon! She'd be able to make pies and tarts aplenty. It would be good to dry as many as possible, too. The grapes were fresh, but they'd soon grow moldy. If the days stayed warm, she could dry them in the sun. Raisins would taste fine during the winter months.

Lettering on the staves of the single firkin read MO–LASS–ES. *Molasses!* But nine gallons of it? Brewers in the New World made rum from molasses, but surely nine gallons of the stuff wouldn't yield enough to make the effort worthwhile. Then again, what household would require an entire firkin of it?

Four jugs clanked and rattled against the molasses firkin.

Garnet wondered about their contents. Just about anything could fill them, but if it were spirits, that could bode ill. A drunken man was a mean man. So far, Samuel Walsh had been uncommonly mild and kind. If he drank, that might change in an instant.

"Come up here, Garnet. I'd like you to see the meadow. 'Tis a lovely sight." He reached out a hand and helped her climb over and onto the seat. "Your hand is cold."

She snatched her hand back, then yanked his cloak over her lap and burrowed her hands beneath it.

Master Walsh pointed into the distance. "See there? My neighbor and I come here to hunt each autumn. A deer trail cuts directly through here, so we've gotten several. There's an earnest need for me to do some hunting before winter sets in."

She nodded.

"I have a small smokehouse. It hasn't much in it at the moment. We've eaten through most of our supplies, and they've yet to be replenished. I've been busy with the crops."

Pointing at the flintlock, then the meadow, Garnet struggled to come up with a way to make him understand her. She tapped her chest. Then her thumb and forefinger made a ring, and she pulled the circle across the air and closed it, repeating the action several times.

"You make sausage."

Pleased he understood her, she nodded.

"Venison sausage would taste fine. I'd be most appreciative of you making some."

Garnet bit her sore lip and gingerly reached down. She fleetingly touched the fabric of his britches at the worn knee but withdrew her fingers as if they had been burnt. Steeling herself with a deep breath, she then made a sewing motion.

"You'd make me buckskin breeches?"

Her head bobbed once again. She held up two fingers and branched her hands over her head to make a rack of antlers.

Samuel boomed out a great laugh. "You talk well with those hands, girl. Two deer to make the buckskins. I know how to tan hides. I already have one all cured."

She wrinkled her nose.

"Aye, the process stinks. I'll do so away from the house."

His house. I can ask about his house. Garnet shaded her eyes and pretended to look around, then sketched a shape in the air.

"You see a cabin."

She pointed at him.

"Ah. Where is my home? We'll travel 'til a little past noon. That'll be at the Mortons'. They're my nearest neighbors. Our homes lie about a mile apart."

She eased back and quietly watched the scenery. Other than the road, no sign of civilization existed. Back home in England, cottages and farms dotted the landscape. She hadn't traveled more than from her own village to her husband's, but that trip took only half a morning. She'd seen habitations aplenty during the transit, too. Garnet couldn't figure out a way to ask how late in the day they'd left the small town yesterday, but all of their travels since then carried them past untamed land.

This is called the New World. I thought it received that name because it was newly discovered. Maybe that's not so. Perhaps it's because coming here causes a person to start life afresh because it is all so different.

❧

Sam was glad of the silence between them now. If there happened to be any game, sound would make it bolt. He'd mentioned the need to replenish the meat supply. Though Garnet might not speak aloud, she could make noise. She remained quiet, and he stayed vigilant.

Once past the meadow, Samuel looked down at Garnet and frowned. Her hand felt like ice earlier. Now shivers wracked her. He resisted the urge to touch the backs of his fingers to her forehead to test her for a fever. She happened to turn toward him and looked up. Her heat-flushed cheek told him she'd contracted a fever. Glassy eyes and chattering teeth reinforced his diagnosis, yet she did her best to smile bravely and straightened up.

Sam didn't have the heart to remark on her ill health. Instead, he pulled the heavy woolen garment she'd draped over her lap earlier. "Let's wrap you." He draped it around her slight frame.

Awhile later, the wagon drew up to the front of a farm-house. A girl of middling school years ran up. "Heaven have mercy! Goodman Walsh, you've a woman with you!"

"God's blessings, Mary Morton. Go fetch your mother."

He eased away from Garnet. She'd fallen asleep again, and he'd tucked her close to his side in hopes of warming her sufficiently. She'd not been cold in the least, though. Once he got off the wagon, he gathered Garnet into his arms.

"Samuel!" Ruth Morton exited her cabin as she wiped her hands on the edge of her apron. "Mary told me you'd brought home a woman."

"Ruth, I fear she's ailing. I'll bear her to the barn so we don't take sickness into the house."

Ruth drew closer and parted the cloak so she could assess the situation. "Mary, you and Henry tote the tub to the barn. Fill it halfway with water from the pump. John, fetch the boiling kettle and bring it, carefully, mind you. Peter, fetch my bedgown and a blanket. Hubert, bring a towel and soap."

Hubert tugged on his mother's skirt. "Master Walsh said she's sick, Mama—not dirty."

"Yes, dearie. I know. But she can't sweat away her fever if dirt covers her."

"I'll fetch the soap!"

"And a towel," Ruth called.

Sam laid Garnet on the blanket Ruth spread on the barn floor. He thought to leave, but Ruth stopped him. "Wait 'til I bathe her face. If she rouses with strangers, she'll be frightened."

Her words made perfect sense. Samuel hunkered down and snatched the soggy cloth from Ruth. "Go ahead and start on her slippers and stockings." He gently swiped Garnet's face a few times.

"I've not seen such filth on a person before," Ruth stated in a hushed tone as she removed the girl's slippers. They were nearly worn through at the soles. "Dear me, she's even worse off than I thought."

Samuel shoved up Garnet's sleeves and swiped at her arms and wrists. "Cooling her will help."

Ruth struggled with the knot in the waist tape of Garnet's skirts. "Talk to her, Sam. I don't want her waking to think someone means her harm."

Samuel dipped the cloth again and rubbed it across Garnet's forehead. "Open your eyes, Garnet. Wake now."

Garnet remained alarmingly limp and silent.

Ruth clucked over Garnet's bodice. "Oh, such care she took making this. The buttonholes—she embroidered little flowers about them. I doubt I'll ever manage to salvage these clothes, Samuel. They're rags."

"If you're concerned about saving her clothes, am I to assume you're sure you can spare her life?"

"How she fares is in God's hands. She's half starved and in a deep swoon." Ruth sat back on her heels and thought for a moment. "I'm going to have you lift her so I can remove her bodice and loosen her shirt. Once that's done, you can leave. I'll sponge her off since she hasn't roused."

Ruth's plan seemed practical enough. Garnet would remain modestly covered. Samuel scooped Garnet into his arms and lifted her. She let out a whimper, and he immediately cupped her head to his shoulder and made a shushing sound.

"God bless her." Compassion whispered in Ruth's prayer. She looked up and gave him a quizzical look. "How did you come by her?"

He rasped, "I bought her in town. She cannot speak."

"You bought her?"

"Look how pitiful she is. Her owner was cruel, and I couldn't bear to leave her with him." He changed his hold to allow Ruth to unbutton the homespun waistcoat from the base of Garnet's throat down to a very narrow waist. The garment was a standard woman's article, simply and modestly made. But even with layers of clothing beneath it, Garnet still looked impossibly thin.

"Alas, Samuel, your heart is compassionate—"

"I confess, 'twas not just an act of mercy, Ruth. I'm hoping she'll stay so I can get Hester back from Dorcas. It grieves me deeply to have my daughter under her roof."

Ruth nodded. "She's a difficult one. Still, how are you to. . ." Her voice trailed off, and she gasped as the waistcoat came free and the back of the shirt beneath it sagged. "Oh, Sam!"

five

He didn't mean to look, but he couldn't help himself. He reflexively held Garnet closer and glanced down. Ruth's hands shook as they unfastened the last few lacings, but the fabric stuck to ugly wounds. Garnet's back bore lash marks and bruises aplenty. For a brief second, she roused only enough to stiffen and whimper before her body wilted.

"Blessed Savior, have mercy," Samuel whispered in anguished prayer.

Ruth swallowed hard. "Rise up and hold her for me, Sam. I thought to leave her on the blanket and sponge her clean, but I must soak the shift to peel it from the stripes on her back."

"Aye, then. Be quick about this ere she rouses. I tell you, Ruth, I didn't know she was wounded. She bore her pain in silence." Sam tucked one arm behind Garnet's knees and rose.

Ruth removed each garment until the strange woman wore only her threadbare shift. Samuel supported Garnet's weight, but in no way did he help divest her of a single scrap of cloth. He wouldn't shame her or himself in such manner, so he kept his eyes trained on a dusty cobweb hanging from a nearby rafter.

"There now." Ruth moved away. "Lower her into the water. The tub's a little to your left and a pace and a half ahead."

The toe of his boot let him know he'd found the large wooden vat. Water saturated his sleeves as he gently folded

Garnet and situated her in the tub.

"It'll take some time to soak the shirt away from her wounds. Send Mary in with more buckets of water. We may as well see to the girl's hair. You called her Garnet, did you not?"

"Aye. Garnet Wheelock. She's a widow. Sold to cover her husband's debts."

"Best you and Falcon pray, Samuel. By faith, I say only the Almighty can heal the wounds in the heart of a woman so miserably mistreated."

Sam exited the barn. The Morton children all crowded around to hear about Garnet. Sam heaved a sigh. "Mary, your mother requires your assistance. John and Henry, round up buckets. They'll need more water."

"Samuel!" Falcon, Ruth's husband, came from a nearby field with Hubert riding on his shoulders. "My son tells me you brought back a woman."

"He did, Father," John shouted. "But she's sick."

Mary gave John and Henry each a shove. "Hush and go fetch water. Father needs to speak with Goodman Walsh."

Falcon lowered Hubert to the ground and ruffled his hair. "I spied a few hens by the oak stump. Take Peter, and search for eggs."

"Peter!" Hubert scampered off.

Falcon's jaunty grin faded. "So the woman's ill?"

Sam nodded curtly. "A fever's taken hold. Ruth's with her. I didn't know when I bought her that she'd been whipped."

Falcon turned toward Samuel. "What, my friend, could have possibly motivated you to buy a bride?"

"She's not to be my bride." The very notion appalled him.

Falcon shook his head. "After years of rearing the children on your own, I fail to understand this."

Sam folded his arms akimbo. "My reason is plain enough. I'm not rearing my children; I'm rearing my sons."

"Ahh, Hester."

"I want my daughter back, and I cannot pry her from Dorcas unless I have capable assistance. I confess, after realizing Garnet's ill, I think perhaps I have lost my fair reason."

Falcon slapped him on the shoulder. "I doubt this. The hand of our Lord moves in unexpected ways. We should trust in His wisdom instead of your understanding. My goodwife will tend the girl with care."

Falcon's faith—both in God and his wife's skill—reassured Sam. "How have my sons fared?"

"They're fine boys. Hardworking. They missed you sorely, though. Your Christopher and my Aaron have done well, going to and fro your place each morning and eve. I sent Ethan with them this noon with instructions for the boys to divert water from the stream into your watering pond. I figure our flocks can graze in your pasture the next week or so."

Sam frowned. "My sheep haven't overgrazed, have they?"

"They ate no more than I expected." Falcon gestured dismissively. "Your land sustained my sheep when I took my grain to the mill. I daresay our flocks could double in size and still have sufficient pasture. I see you have a turkey in your wagon."

"My trip turned out to be far more productive than I expected. I've apples and grapes to share."

"I'll not turn down either. 'Twill be good to enjoy them."

Samuel heard laughter and pivoted. "Christopher! Ethan!"

His sons rounded a bend of trees. At the sound of his voice, they ran into his outstretched arms. At thirteen, Christopher was a copy of his father. Tall and broad, he would soon be a man. Ten and already stretching past the phase where he was nothing more than knees and elbows, Ethan showed the same promise.

Samuel hugged them both, then stated matter-of-factly, "I've brought a woman home. Her name is Widow Wheelock. She's ailing, but as soon as she recovers, she'll help us greatly."

Christopher asked, "Are you going to marry her, Father?"

Falcon chuckled. "You can't fault him, Samuel. All will wonder the selfsame thing."

"They'd do better to mind their own business than to plot out my life." Sam gave his sons a steady look. "I bought the widow so we can bring Hester home."

Falcon peered over Sam's shoulder and raised his brows as Mary emerged from the barn and approached them.

"Father, Mama's rubbing the lady's hair dry. She directed me to tell you the woman's fever is because she's hurt, not because she bears disease."

"She's hurt?" Ethan scratched his elbow.

Sam didn't want to explain. "Goodwife Morton's seeing to the widow. You boys go gather your belongings." As the boys walked away, Sam and Falcon turned and headed to the barn. Falcon called out, and Ruth softly bade them enter. Sam strode to the edge of the blanket and hunkered down. "How does she fare, Ruth?"

Ruth finished wrapping the towel about Garnet's hair and whispered in a pained tone, "No one ought ever be so mistreated."

Falcon rested his hand on her shoulder. "She won't be again."

"She's not roused at all. Perchance she ought to remain here for a time."

Samuel's face tightened. "I understand you mean her well, but she's been bought and sold twice already. To finally awaken and discover herself in yet another household will only make matters worse. I'll take the boys and go on home with her."

Ruth chewed on her lip for a moment. "I suppose you can keep watch over her whilst Christopher goes to Dorcas's and fetches Hester."

Sam shook his head. "I'll need to fetch my daughter."

Falcon nodded. "A wise decision. For all her sour talk, Dorcas benefits from keeping your daughter. With Hester carding wool, Dorcas is able to spin far more. She'll be loath to let Hester go."

"The decision isn't hers to make. Hester's my daughter. She's coming home."

"Your resolve is clear." Falcon addressed his wife. "Dear, Sam offered us some apples and grapes. Go see to having the children carry in whatever Sam spares us. Mary can stay with the widow whilst I empty the water into the garden."

Ruth rose. "Come, Samuel. We'll prepare a place in your wagon. Feed her broth until I pay a call in a day or two. Mind you, give her nothing more than broth or hasty pudding. Curds and whey are acceptable, as well. She's too careworn to take in much else."

"I'm thankful for your skill." They reached the wagon. He looked at the apples and grapes. "I'll leave a basket of apples and most of the grapes for your family. The grapes will spoil ere Garnet's healed sufficiently to dry them."

"I'll take just a few apples and thank you for the grapes. In a few days, I'll come to call and help Garnet preserve apples. 'Twill provide an excuse for me to come, so I'll tend her back again then. She'll be able to stay seated whilst we work on the apples afterward."

Ruth called to one of the children. It took no time at all for her to fill the baskets they brought from the house with grapes and apples. She took Christopher and Ethan's blankets and formed a bed for Garnet.

Falcon came out of the barn with the little widow in his arms. Samuel barely kept from gaping. Completely washed and clean, Garnet wore a white linen bedgown. His cloak wrapped about her at least twice over. Fever painted bright red flags across her cheeks. Even so, her finely carved features relaxed with sleep into a rare prettiness. Without caked-on mud and grease, her hair took his breath away. Her name made perfect sense now, because her tresses were a deep, rich red.

Ruth fussed with the cloak as Falcon put Garnet in the wagon.

"Falcon, you're blessed to have such a good woman to wife."

"I know. I think it a shame you've not yet found another woman for your hearth."

"I cannot imagine marrying again. It would not be a good union."

Ruth cast her husband an exasperated look. "The topic's come up before and will yet again. For now, take pity on this woman and let Sam take her home. Sam, put her abed and keep her there. If the fever stays high, you know how to brew willow bark."

"I will."

"Go with God."

❧

Garnet woke and slowly studied her surroundings. She lay in a jump bed, propped up by several pillows. Half-drawn bed curtains kept the heat radiating from a low fire in the hearth. Hazy memories of a little girl singing to her and a man giving her sips of water filtered through her mind. The last thing she clearly remembered was plucking a turkey as she sat at the back of the man's wagon. The man—his name was Wa-something. *Walter? Wallace? Walsh. Yes. Walsh. Am I in his home?*

She couldn't bring herself to stay abed at all, let alone in a stranger's home. Garnet pushed off the thick coverlet and swung her legs over the side of the bed. She felt a little dizzy, but that passed soon enough. A neatly made trundle poked halfway out from beneath the bed. Nicely enough, it acted like a step for her. She paused a moment again as dizziness assailed her, then shoved the trundle in the rest of the way.

Her master's keeping room looked spare. Aside from a few trunks and the cupboard, it held only the bed, a table, and benches. As homes went, this one wasn't cluttered, but it certainly wasn't clean, either. Many of the things Garnet expected were absent. No herbs hung on the ceiling pegs to dry. Neither did many vegetables dehydrate on shelves, racks, or pegs. The posts for drying apple rings lay barren. The clarified hide that served as a window wore such a thick coat of dust, no light filtered in.

Worried her master might enter when she wore only a nightdress, Garnet searched for something to lend a little modesty. A length of cloth lay draped over a peg, so she helped herself to it, tying it into a petticoat of sorts. With a towel for a shawl, she looked passably covered.

The fire burned too low in the large stone fireplace. Garnet added another log and checked the pot that simmered over the flames. The broth inside held no flavoring save the remainder of what she suspected to be the turkey Samuel had shot on their travel homeward. A few stale crusts of bread lay sprinkled across the tabletop. She dusted off the far end of the table, helped herself to a bowl, and soon had corn bread ready to bake. After putting the cast-iron pan over the fire, Garnet took one of the carrots and a turnip, chopped them, and added both to the broth.

"You're up!"

six

Garnet turned and smiled at the young girl she faintly remembered. The little dark-haired beauty stood in the doorway, clutching a basket of eggs. "Father says you must rest yet. I am Hester."

Garnet wet her lips and lightly shook her head. She looked down at her ridiculous outfit and plucked at it, then smiled at the girl as her brows rose in question.

"Papa says Goodwife Morton has your overgarments. She's to come today. You'll like her. She has a merry heart and will be glad to see you're better." She put the basket down and smoothed her apron. "I'm to go gather feathers. You'll not get me into trouble by doing much, will you?"

Garnet gave her a smile and shooed her away. Waves of weariness washed over her, but she couldn't very well lie back down. Instead, she sat at the table, took up a knife, and very carefully peeled all of the candle wax from the candlesticks into a small plate. She felt terribly weak, but she desperately wanted to be useful. Moments later, a shadow fell over her.

"Good morrow, Garnet Wheelock! You'll not recall me. I'm Ruth Morton—Samuel Walsh's neighbor to the south. I hope you'll be my friend, as well as my neighbor."

Garnet rose as the woman began to speak and curtsied.

"Oh, don't fuss with that. Sit down. Better yet, you ought to lie down. I didn't expect you to be up. You still belong abed."

Garnet didn't want to be quarrelsome, but she shook her head.

Ruth smiled. "I'll have to trouble my mind now whether to leave you the overgarments you wore, for I fear to do so will enable you to stay up. We want only good for you."

Her face was so preciously kind that Garnet felt something deep inside start to crack. Something about Ruth's steady blue eyes and soft voice made her feel so vulnerable. All she'd endured suddenly loomed up and nearly overwhelmed her. She found herself clasped to a soft, ample bosom, rocked, and crooned to as if she were but a babe.

When Garnet's weeping drew to a conclusion, Ruth simply brushed a kiss on her forehead and whispered, "A good cry is ofttimes what a body needs most to return to health."

Abashed, Garnet nodded and went to get the pan of corn bread from the fire. She stirred the broth and couldn't help making a face at it.

Ruth twittered. "I oft wonder that Sam and the children don't get the dwindles. He cooks only the most basic of necessities. Christopher chars meat over the fire when he must. Little Hester just came home, and I fear she's too small to trust much near the fireplace."

Garnet nodded in acknowledgment. Not wanting to ridicule her benefactor for the lack of staples in his home, Garnet still needed to know about the food supplies. She pointed to the ceiling. The meager supply of herbs and vegetables spoke for itself.

" 'Tis harvesttime, and there's a need to dry and put up. You've actually a well-planted garden, and God was generous this year. Samuel left the grapes at my farm. I've set them out to dry in the sun and charged my sons to keep the birds away from them. We'll share the raisins betwixt our homes. In a day or two, I'll return, and we'll preserve your apples."

Garnet found herself smiling at the woman.

"Here, now. Let me see to your marks."

She knows about them?

"Don't fuss," Ruth said gently. "Someone mistreated you, and 'twas to his shame—not yours. Christ was whipped, too—and we know He was innocent."

This woman wants to be my friend. How blessed I am that You've given me her, Lord.

Ruth Morton smiled. "If I'm pleased with how you're healing, I'll allow you the overgarments. I fear, should I not, you might be seen gardening in a bedgown!"

Garnet smiled.

Ruth took care of her back, helped her dress, and chattered the whole time. "Samuel Walsh is a widower. His wife's been in her grave almost five years now. The only man I know who's kinder than Samuel is my husband, Falcon." Ruth laughed. "I'm partial to Falcon, so the comparison is a compliment."

Garnet smiled, then held out her hand and drew imaginary stair steps in the air, then flipped both hands palm upward and raised her brows.

"Children?" Ruth reached up and adjusted the clout covering her hair. "Samuel has three. Two sons and little Hester. All three are well behaved."

Garnet gestured again.

"Yes, the dear Lord has blessed Falcon and me. We have four sons and a daughter. There were two more children, but they returned to God's bosom. Have you had children?"

Garnet shook her head.

"I'd planned to make corn pone and split pea soup while

here, but I can see you've already seen to the meal. Rest, Garnet."

Garnet waved to encompass the entire keeping room.

Ruth laughed. "I can't deny that much wants doing here. Samuel is a kind man, though. He wouldn't expect you to work for a while yet. Plenty of time lies ahead for you to put your hand to tasks."

Though she opened her mouth, no sound came out. Garnet wanted so badly to talk to Ruth Morton. The love of God shone in her kind eyes.

"Sam told me you're mute, yet you speak in your sleep."

Sadly, Garnet hitched her shoulder. She didn't understand the malady, either.

"Mayhap the Lord is permitting you this trial to increase your faith. Some religious orders practice silence." Ruth smiled. "When God is ready, He'll give you back your voice. Betwixt then and now, we'll manage. Now I'm going to take my leave. I'll be back day after next. Rest up, because I aim to have us dry apples and make applesauce. 'Twill be a busy day."

Ruth gave her a hug and paused ere she stepped over the threshold. "When the boys stayed with me, they brought over the milk each day. I churned butter aplenty and tucked some in your springhouse."

Garnet hurried over to the doorway.

"Oh, you've not gone outside yet? Come." Ruth took her arm and led her off to the left. "The stream here flows with sweet water. Sam built a springhouse off to the side so you can keep butter, milk, and eggs even during the hottest part of the summer."

After looking at the clever setup and feeling a spurt of gratitude that she wouldn't have to haul water far at all,

Garnet looked back at the house. She shot Ruth a startled look and held up two fingers.

"Aye. The boys sleep on the second level. 'Tis a common arrangement in these parts. The entrance is on the other side and can only be reached by a ladder. Winters are bitterly cold. This way, the fire's heat remains down in the keeping room. If memory serves me correctly, Sam cut a trapdoor in the floor so the upstairs can take on some heat before he sends the boys to bed."

Tapping her temple, Garnet smiled.

"Aye, 'tis clever. I'll be back day after tomorrow."

Garnet dipped another curtsy. Ruth had called her a friend and been exceedingly kind, but Garnet knew Samuel was not only master of the house but her master, as well. She would thank him for rescuing her and for his kindness by serving his family with diligence.

❧

Samuel plucked a weed and stood back up. "God's blessing on you, Ruth."

"I've just come from visiting Garnet. She fares well enough."

"Fie! She needs rest yet."

"You'll not see it of her. Already, she's made corn bread and worries over the harvest. She was modest when I tended her. What do you know of her?"

Sam knew Ruth was no gossip. Her interest stemmed from Christian charity. He leaned on his hoe. "I know nothing other than her name and that she's a widow. I'm heartened to hear you think her health's improved."

"The girl has a ways to go, but time will solve that."

"It bodes well that she's modest. I've never seen sadder eyes, but the cause is unknown to me. Sorrow of all kinds can dim the spirit in such a way."

Ruth tucked her hands into the pocket of her apron. "The marks on her back bode ill. Have you considered that she may be with child?"

Necessity made such frank talk acceptable. Still, Samuel squinted at the horizon. "I've no way of knowing. Time will tell. Hester shares the jump bed. Any offspring won't be mine."

"Samuel Walsh! I would have never supposed that to be the case!"

He gave Ruth a grin. "You might not, but others can be quick to judge and slow to think. I appreciate the faith you carry for me."

"Hear me: I know you too well to think otherwise. Her overgarments are in tatters. If you still have Naomi's old things, I'm sure Garnet would not take offense if you offered them."

"They're in the barn. I'll fetch them."

Ruth looked down at the rich earth and said softly, "Just because they're the same clothes doesn't mean the woman wearing them will take on the same temperament. I probably ought not speak ill of the dead, but memories of your wife. . ." Her voice died out as she shrugged.

Sam nodded curtly. He'd been careful not to speak of his wife. The memories were unpleasant at best. His sons didn't need to hear tales of a shrewish mother, and they'd been young enough to be unaware of Naomi's worst qualities. Sam refused to lie about her, so silence was the best he could manage.

"I meant you no insult, Samuel. I intended to give reassurance, not to gossip."

Sam shifted his weight. "Truth is the truth. I didn't for

a moment question your motive. You and your husband have been stalwart friends. 'Twas a merciful thing you said, for I confess, I hesitated to fetch Naomi's clothing for that ridiculous fear."

"You couldn't help it, Sam. Your memories are painful ones."

"There are those who would fault a man for living by feeling instead of faith." He cleared his throat.

"You? Lack of faith? Oh, Sam! You've acted wisely. A man shouldn't plunge back into the river when he almost drowned in it."

His face and ears burned. As a man with children, his family rated higher on a level of need than did a single man. Twice, though, he'd refused bridal candidates. The first time, the woman's father asserted he expected Samuel to give over Christopher in exchange. The second had been last summer—but Sam recoiled from the very notion of taking the offered thirteen-year-old bride.

Ruth took her hands out of the pocket of her apron. "Who knows? Mayhap you waited because the Lord had Garnet in store for you."

He stared at Ruth, and his voice went rough. "Put aside that thinking here and now."

Ruth laughed. "Now, Sam, there's no need to get riled. You've brought your daughter home and have a woman there."

"I'll move my bed to the attic to still any wagging tongues and quench wild imaginations."

"You'll do no such thing—at least not yet! The trundle is decent enough until Garnet has recovered. If Garnet's fever returns, Hester is too small to go outside and climb up a ladder in the pitch dark of night. Clearly, these are uncommon circumstances. With the bed curtains closed between the trundle and the jump bed, along with little Hester there, propriety is maintained."

"It's a temporary arrangement. As soon as I'm positive she's fully recovered, I'll join my sons in the loft."

"You've thought it out. I agree with the plan. For you to stay in the keeping room would make others believe you're fostering an attraction."

He scowled. "Widow Wheelock is comely, but her character is yet a mystery. I know nothing of her. I've not even heard her voice other than in the garbled mutterings of a fever."

"You might think to have the reverend pray over her. That she talks in the night means her heart is sorely troubled. No doubt, he will pay a call to see her. The elders will demand it."

"I assumed it to be the case. They'll see her on the Sabbath."

"Best you be sure to give her Naomi's cap. Her hair is a thing of beauty and will be cause for comment. She's not vain in the least, but others will find it less than plain. To have an attractive widow under your roof will likely wreak havoc."

Samuel mulled over Ruth's words for the rest of the morning. At midday, he went to the cabin for lunch. Corn bread awaited him, fragrant and still warm. Hester met him in the doorway, her eyes twinkling. She whispered excitedly, "Just imagine! She fixed up the broth!"

A bouquet of mustard and sweet cicely poked out of a small crock on the table. A small bundle of the same lay off to the side on one of the trunks. Herbs and flowers hadn't been brought into the cabin since Naomi died four years before—and then they'd been for use and never to simply add charm to their abode.

In deference to the small woman who had fallen fast asleep on the bed once again, Sam silenced his sons as they entered the house. They sat down, and Samuel ladled up the soup. His mouth began to water. A few sliced cabbage leaves floated along with the carrot and turnip bits. The broth was thickened with something to give it body, and bits of seasonings that teased his memory lent a toothsome aroma to the steam rising from the pot. Best of all, dumplings floated on the surface.

"Did she make this, or did Ruth Morton?" Ethan demanded to know in a hiss of a whisper.

Hester smiled and giggled as she pointed to the small occupant of the jump bed. "She did."

As Christopher reached to help himself to even more, Samuel checked his arm and inquired, "Did she partake of any, Hester?"

"Aye. Only the littlest bit."

Samuel let go of Christopher's arm and let him have more. "She eats very little."

"She's not much larger than Ethan," Christopher decided, staring at the small form on the bed. "Are you sure she's all grown up?"

Samuel hadn't thought to ask her age. One didn't ask such a thing, but under the circumstances, it was an understandable question. Christopher counted thirteen winters, and he'd wish to marry in another three or four years. He was coming to the point that young bucks noticed women. Still, Samuel had held her and knew she was not in the bud but in the bloom of her life.

"Mayhap when she awakens, we can discover more of her."

They finished eating and went back out. Samuel returned

to the house past sunset. Hester sat outside the door and churned butter. "Father, we've been busy!"

"Is that so?" He paused and relished the happiness lighting his daughter's face.

Her head bobbed in rhythm with the knocking paddle. "The lady took me for a little walk. We gathered milkweed and twisted it. She told me it'll serve as candlewicks."

"She's talking?"

"With her hands," Hester said in a blithe tone. "Ethan caught fish. Three fish. The lady is making them for supper."

"So that's what smells so good."

Garnet lightly fried the fish in butter and sprinkled fresh dill over them. She also sliced, fried, and seasoned potatoes. A salad of freshly picked dandelion greens filled up the remainder of the space on the pewter plates. Christopher poked Ethan in the side and mocked, "It's about time you caught good-tasting fish!"

"What is this?" Samuel looked at an odd thing in the center of the table.

"You'll never imagine, Father. We looked about, and there are only a few tapers left. Widow Wheelock scraped the wax from the candlesticks and melted it on a plate. She dipped mullein leaves in it."

Sure enough, as supper almost ended and the room got dim, Garnet lit the tip of the leaf, and it acted just like a candle.

"You're clever, Garnet. I've not seen such a thing. I'll have Ethan gather rushes from the stream on the morrow. They make good light, too."

She nodded and got up to clear the table.

"Garnet, Hester will clear the table. I need you to sit back down. I'll ask you about yourself. Ethan, fetch your slate for us."

Garnet hesitantly sat down.

"Without a formal introduction, we've done well thus far," Samuel moderated. "But the time has come to discover a bit more about you. Forgive my lack of manners, but I wish to know your age."

She held up all ten fingers, then closed her hands for a second before holding all of them up again.

"Twenty. The man I bought you from said you were sold to pay your husband's debts. Am I correct in presuming your husband died?"

She nodded.

Obviously, she was remembering something painful. Samuel gave her a few moments. "When the time came that your mourning was over, did you hold an understanding with someone to become his wife?"

She decisively shook her head.

"I am Samuel, as I told you. I am nine and twenty. My wife died four years past. Christopher is thirteen; Ethan, ten; and Hester is five." He felt it necessary to impart that information so she'd have a chance to collect herself. Judging by her wide eyes, short, quick breaths, and tightly clasped hands, Garnet was rattled. He should have told her about his family as they traveled. She must have been frightened, coming into an unknown situation. Just because she couldn't speak didn't mean that she didn't communicate.

"I should have thought to spin yarns about the children on our journey. You'll learn of them soon enough, though. They are good children and most often do their chores willingly. I've not had much trouble from them and do not anticipate that you shall, either. Nevertheless, you've my leave to bid them do whatever chores you deem necessary."

Her lips parted in surprise, then pressed together as she dipped her head. Did she think he was teasing or ridiculing her? He barely grazed the back of her hand. "Heed me, Widow Wheelock. I redeemed you unto yourself. I've need of help and hope you will consent to stay, but I'll not have you to slave, nor will my children show you disrespect. Freedom is a right in this land. I'll not hold with denying it to another."

He saw the shock in her face and tried to continue as if he'd not said anything to surprise her. To make an issue of her emancipation would be more of an emotional drain, and he wanted to discover as much as possible about her past. That, in and of itself, was going to be hard enough.

Her hands shook as she took the slate he placed in them. He fought the urge to steady them. Instead, he wove his fingers together and rested his clasped hands on the tabletop. "Are you able to read and write?"

She held her thumb and forefinger apart.

Samuel stated softly, "A little. That's better than I could have hoped. If you'd care to learn more, mayhap I could teach you in the evenings. Without speech, you need some way to talk. I understand you've not spoken to anyone since your ship landed, yet you do in your sleep. Won't you speak to us now?"

Her lower lip quavered pathetically, and she captured it between her teeth. He hadn't noticed until now that her front teeth overlapped ever so slightly. That small flaw was strangely endearing. Tears slipped down her cheeks, and she closed her eyes to dam them in.

"I'm a patient man. When you're ready, you'll speak. Until then, we'll get by. You seem much at home on a farm." He spoke in a carefully modulated tone, trying to elicit information without fraying her composure more than necessary. "I take it your family farmed?"

She nodded jerkily.

"Well and good. Indeed, that is well and good! We are in sore need of a woman's help and influence. Believe me, your knowledge and skills will be more than welcome. My little Hester could be merry to have a lady friend."

Garnet looked over at the little girl and gave her a ghost of a smile. Samuel knew that smile cost her dearly. She was obviously grief-stricken, yet she cared enough about a child's feelings to try to set aside her own hurts for a moment.

"Because you now abide with us, I fetched Hester home. My wife died the year after bearing Hester. Dorcas—my wife's sister—has kept Hester for me since then."

Hester gave Garnet's arm an exuberant hug. "I like you. And I know you like me. Aunt Dorcas is sour as unripe berries."

Samuel cleared his throat.

Hester shot him a surprised look. "Aunt Dorcas always says it's not gossiping if what she tells is the truth."

"It's not a lie if you're telling the truth," he said slowly. "But if your reason for telling a truth is to make someone else think badly of another, then you've stooped to gossiping."

Hester beamed at him. "Then I wasn't sinful, Father. I was telling Widow Wheelock a happy truth. She is kind and cares nicely for me. It is a good change."

Garnet gave Hester a smile and pressed a trencher into her small hands. Hester headed for the swill bucket to scrape off the scraps. The young widow arched her brow at him.

Samuel cast a look at his precious little daughter, then measured his words carefully. "I owe Dorcas a debt of gratitude for the safety she afforded Hester. Dangers abound, and I couldn't mind her adequately on my own. Hester is capable of helping about the house and assisted Dorcas in many ways."

Garnet's brow puckered. Since she sat with her back to Hester, she crossed her arms in a huglike fashion and rocked from side to side.

Samuel answered her with a curt shake, then forced his voice to sound positive. "As Hester said, 'tis clear your heart overflows with affection. Having her back and knowing she will flourish under your care—'tis undoubtedly a heavenly reply to countless, diligent prayers."

Her eyes misted, and she again crossed her arms and made a silent pledge to cherish Hester.

"You have my gratitude." He paused, then pressed on. "What do I need to know about you? Did you leave any children behind?"

Garnet shook her head, and he let out a gusty sigh of relief. "Good. Very good. I've noticed you pray. Is this of habit or of heart?"

Her hand went to her bosom and patted over her heart. Suddenly, her features twisted with revulsion. She shoved away from the table and inched backward.

seven

Samuel turned around to see what elicited such a strong reaction from Garnet. He saw nothing out of the ordinary. A bit of movement caught his eye. A field mouse scampered along the edge of the room and darted toward the broom. He turned back and realized Garnet's gaze remained pinned on the creature. " 'Tis naught but a field mouse and a babe at that, Garnet. Chris, grab the broom and sweep him out."

Garnet opened the door, and Sam thought it helpful of her; but as Christopher started to nudge the mouse, Garnet lost all color and shuddered dramatically. The tiny rodent scampered toward freedom, and Garnet let out a wail. She spun around and raced outside.

The dark swallowed her when she was a few feet away, but her terrified screaming made her easy to track. For one so sick and weak, she moved with astonishing swiftness. Samuel chased after her and tackled her in the middle of what had recently been his cornfield. Even though small and pitifully frail, she fought him wildly—kicking, scratching, and hitting with panicked desperation.

"Garnet! Garnet!" He tried to calm her, but she'd spiraled completely out of control. Samuel hated to strike her, but he knew no other way. He slapped her cheek, and her screaming halted in the middle of a shrill note. She sucked in a shocked breath, then broke into body-wracking sobs.

"Garnet, Garnet." He wrapped her up in his arms and

rocked her in the field of dirt and cornstalks. Her hands fisted, clenching his clothing in tight balls as she pressed her cheek to his chest and wept. He pulled her closer still and murmured wordless sounds of comfort. It tore at him to witness her raw horror. He'd failed to appreciate the depth of her fear, a mistake he'd not make again.

"Father?" Christopher shuffled close by. He held one of her candle leaves.

"Light us back, son." Samuel stood and cradled her in his arms. Wrenching sobs still shook her tiny frame all the way back to the house. Hester stood in the doorway, gnawing uncertainly on her knuckles.

Christopher patted Garnet's arm. "It's gone. I got rid of it."

Sam ordered softly, "Hester, you'll aid me with Garnet. Boys, you'd best wait outside." Hester silently helped him tuck the woman in bed.

Garnet finally reached the point of total exhaustion. Her tears and energy spent, she lay facing the wall with a dull look that carried hopelessness and heartache. Sam gently smoothed back her hair. "Hester, curl beside her here in the bed. The widow needs the warmth of another's presence and caring."

Samuel tucked his daughter in and watched as she turned and wound her arms around Garnet and nestled close. "We'll love you, Garnet," Hester whispered in her soft, pure voice. "You can be here with me and Father and Christopher and Ethan. All is well now."

Garnet gave no reaction.

Sam stooped and pressed a kiss on Hester's crown. "Well said. You cuddle and find the peace of a sound rest."

He stepped outside afterward and stared up at the stars.

He sought a second of solace from heaven, but it was slow in coming. Christopher somberly stated, "Mama cried like that once."

Ethan didn't remember his mother. "She did? When?"

"When Grandmother died."

"Did she scream like the demons had her, too?" Ethan asked, his voice shaking with fright.

"Nay." Samuel drew his son close to his side and gave him a reassuring squeeze. "I was there to hold and comfort her. She wept every bit as hard, but she was not alone in her grief."

Christopher kept a bit of distance and tried to act like a young man. He cleared his throat, and his voice barely cracked as he said, "Garnet has no one. Not a soul."

"True. I've no idea what transpired with Garnet, but 'twas something too terrible to let her mind and soul find peace."

Ethan looked up at him. "Father, she has us."

"Aye, that she does, but she barely knows us at all. God, alone, will have to be her comfort until she gains a trust in us."

The boys each recited their scripture for the night, went to the privy, and climbed the ladder to their bed. Samuel went out to the barn and opened a small chest that contained Naomi's clothes. Without discussing the matter, she'd bartered his best ram to obtain a French brocade for her bodice and a length of fancy wool for her skirts. Staunch friends that they were, Falcon Morton and Thomas Brooks both lent him their rams that season. Memory after bitter memory swelled. Samuel tamped them down, grabbed the garments, and shut the chest with notable force. If the Widow Wheelock didn't need the clothing so desperately, he'd have gladly left them tucked away forever.

Sam slipped back into the keeping room. To his relief, Hester and Garnet lay curled together in a warm knot. Hester seemed more than content, but the firelight illuminated Garnet's face. Judging from the expressions flickering there, she suffered troubled dreams.

Unable to change that, Samuel drew the bed curtains closed to keep them warm and provide modesty. He prepared for bed, then pulled the trundle out for himself. The trundle measured far too small for him. Constructed for a pair of small children, it was less than restful for a big man.

That fact didn't matter. Garnet kept him awake with her restless cries. In her sleep, she sobbed and mumbled more pitifully than she had even at the height of her fever.

"Lord most high," Samuel prayed quietly, "take pity on your daughter Garnet. You, alone, know what she's endured. Grant her peace of mind and a tranquil heart."

❧

Garnet surfaced from her sleep in slow degrees, with different things registering one at a time. She was warm. Her back stung. Something felt strangely out of place. She opened her eyes and gasped. .

A large hand rested over hers on the pillow.

Garnet tried to pull away, but that hand curled about hers, and the callous thumb rubbed her palm. "Shh," a deep, slurred voice bade from the other side of the bed curtain.

Her gaze traced from the hand, to the thick, hair-sprinkled wrist, down to the muscled forearm that disappeared between the split of the closed bed curtain. Master Walsh honorably stayed on the trundle, yet he'd sacrificed his comfort and sleep to give her consolation.

Garnet wasn't sure what to do. Part of her wanted to accept

the strength and caring her master offered. On the other hand, a woman of virtue could scarcely allow herself to be in such a compromising position. She made a small sound of protest and tried to slide free of his hold.

"Garnet, rest awhile where you are. You're safe. Daybreak isn't far off."

His tone was so inviting, so mellow that it was impossible to defy his quiet command. She sighed and rubbed her cheek against her pillow. As Samuel Walsh patted her hand, she coasted back to sleep.

The cockerel crowed. At the first rusty sounds the bird made, she came alert. Heat filled her cheeks when she had to disentangle herself from her master's hand.

"Garnet," Samuel ordered, "remain abed whilst I dress. There's no cause for anyone to be overset."

Samuel's bland voice calmed her tremendously. It was his home, and she—she was his rightfully purchased slave. Even so, he'd treated her with respect and great compassion.

Was it just a dream, him telling her that she was free? It was hard to tell fact from fancy anymore. Everything blended in a muddle. Whatever her station in his house, Samuel Walsh seemed to be a godly man. He had not taken advantage of her. That said much of his moral fiber.

In mere moments, the solid sound of him stomping each foot into his boots let her know he'd finished dressing, but a rustling sound ensued.

"Widow Wheelock, hold fast to the bed curtains. I aim to push in the trundle."

He'd made the trundle bed? What manner of man was he, to perform such a mundane, domestic chore? Garnet couldn't answer him, so she simply did as he bade. The trundle scraped a little as he shoved it beneath the jump bed.

"I've placed my wife's clothing upon the table for you. Wear them in good health. I'll go milk the cow. You'll have some privacy." The door opened, then shut.

Garnet crept out of the bed and tucked the covers back over little Hester. Garnet looked down at her tattered clothes. She'd slept in them—a reminder of how she'd panicked the night before. Shame and revulsion washed over her.

I can't waste time regretting what's past. I have to forge ahead and prove myself now.

The luxurious quality of the clothing her master left on the table stunned Garnet. She could scarcely imagine wearing such fine garments. The blue brocade bodice looked fine enough to be worn by the queen's own ladies-in-waiting. The skirts were wool—of mingled blue and green threads—but far more voluminous than a farmer's wife normally wore. With a farthingale beneath them, his wife would have been outfitted elegantly enough to be seen as a woman of consequence in London. The apron was made of finest linen. Never had Garnet owned clothing of this quality, and what she did own bordered on immodest due to its sad condition.

She quickly changed, then knelt at the fire and added just enough wood to bring it to a cooking level. Wood took time to chop and carry. She didn't want to make any more work for the boys. Already familiar with the food supplies on hand, Garnet started corn mush for breakfast. Once she had that underway, she took the larger pot and filled it with a chopped onion, some garlic, half a dozen peppercorns, water, and peas. By nuncheon, she'd locate wild thyme and sage to add to that hearty soup.

Ethan brought in milk, and Christopher filled the wood

box. Those light chores done, they all sat down to eat. After asking the blessing, Samuel added milk to his mush and stirred it. He'd given her clothing a long look, then turned away.

He must have loved his wife dearly to have provided such finery for her. *If seeing me dressed in her clothing is painful, then it would be best for me to change back.*

"Ethan, you're to gather rushes and reeds today. Christopher, you're to stack the cornstalks so they'll finish drying. Another thing: I've seen several hares."

"I'll set snares." Christopher reached across the table, scooped a generous heap of butter with his spoon, and plopped it atop his mush. Grinning at Garnet, he said, "I'm partial to roast hare."

She smiled at his boldness. Ruth Morton had mentioned the Walshes hadn't eaten well in years, and the zeal with which they dug into what she'd prepared made it clear her master and his sons would gladly devour whatever she set before them.

Garnet listened as Master Walsh directed each of the children with their duties. The chores he set out were common enough. She wondered if he was doing this more for her benefit than theirs. Still, it was good of him to let her know how the family operated. She needed to hear what was already set to be accomplished so she could fill in the other areas.

"Widow Wheelock, we are grateful to you for the meal. 'Twas tasty enough, but I'll thank you to remain abed this day. A sickness near took you to the hereafter, and it cannot be permitted to return."

She took up the slate they'd left on the table from last night. Laboriously, she wrote, *I am well.*

He smiled at the way she underlined the last word. "You are spirited, if not completely hale. I fear you will overdo."

Her face scrunched; then she shook her head and used the same gesture she'd used back on the road—of blowing on her hands and a bubble floating away.

Samuel chuckled. "You're right; we have little soap left."

She tapped herself.

"No, no. Soap making will have to wait. You've not enough strength to endure that task. Given a fortnight, I've no doubt but that we'll have soap from your hand. You'll need to save lard up to make it, regardless."

"I'll help make it," Ethan offered. "I've helped Goodwife Morton."

"We'll speak with Ruth Morton. Mayhap you women will labor together over that chore. For this day, Garnet, I'll still thank you to—" He halted midsentence and looked at the message she wrote on the slate.

Work to noon, then rest.

The pleading look she gave made him chuckle. "Very well."

As soon as Hester and she were alone, Garnet changed back into her own clothing. It made no sense to wear such finery as she cleaned this abode. Then, too, mercy demanded she not wear her master's wife's clothing since the sight of it caused him pain.

Garnet paused in the doorway and watched as Christopher stacked the cornstalks so they'd finish drying. His father worked in a distant cornfield, plowing under the stubble. He'd mentioned he needed to do so to restore the soil. Ethan tromped by with an armful of rushes.

Without Hester here, I imagine Master Walsh and his sons

all slept in the keeping room. I cannot continue to usurp his bed. Something must be done, but it isn't for me to determine exactly what. Mayhap, if I air out the bedding, that will nudge him into changing the arrangement.

Garnet beckoned to Ethan. She wrote on the slate, and he laughed. "You want me to throw my bed out?"

Garnet caught the mattress as he tossed it down. As she emptied the ticking, Hester hopped from one foot to the other. "Aunt Dorcas did this, too. I always tied the old corn husks so we could feed the cookfire. Would you have me do that?"

With Hester occupied, Garnet shook out the empty mattress ticking, hung it over a fence, and beat out more dust.

It was obvious from the state of the mattress that the attic desperately needed cleaning. The dirt dislodged when she cleaned the attic would spoil the keeping room in an instant. Best she start up on the second story, then move downstairs later. She took rags, water, and a corn-husk broom up and attacked the attic.

Because the ladder was outside, no room was wasted with a staircase indoors. Both the floors boasted a full measure of usable space. Pegs protruding from the rafters indicated that food and drying once took place up there, too. Since the pegs all stood empty, Garnet set to dispersing a wealth of cobwebs with the broom. She treated the walls with the same vigor, then almost punished the floor to dislodge all of the dried mud.

Mindful of her promise to limit her time, Garnet went down and took the eggs from the morning gathering and whipped up some custard.

As Hester licked the spoon, her eyes brightened. "Are you going to bake it in a pumpkin? Ruth Morton did that once, and Father relished it."

Though unsure as to what a pumpkin was, let alone the peculiarities in using one as a cooking container, Garnet didn't have the heart to deny Hester's request. She nodded.

"I'll go choose the pumpkin!" Hester dashed out the door and returned in a few minutes holding a bright orange squash as big as her head. "I'll scoop out the inside and wash the seeds if you cut it open. I like to eat the roasted seeds."

Pumpkins, turkey, and corn. Virginia Colony provided remarkable food. Garnet filled the hollowed pumpkin with the custard she'd made, then set it inside a cauldron and poured a few inches of water around the edge. Once she hung it over the fire, she picked up a long spoon and prepared to stir the soup.

"I can do that!"

Garnet waggled her forefinger back and forth.

Confusion puckered little Hester's face. "Aunt Dorcas had me stir soups and such."

Women often got nasty burns. Appalled anyone would allow such a small child near a fire, Garnet fought to hide her reaction. Instead, she pointed to the corn husks Hester had tied together and smiled.

"You want me to tie the rest of the husks." Hester plopped back down and set to work. Her nose wrinkled; then she giggled. "Your soup smells better than these old things."

A wink of agreement set Hester into another set of giggles. Garnet added a little more water to the soup and set aside the spoon. She wanted to add thyme and sage, but with no supply of herbs in the house, she feared she'd have no spices whatsoever. A quick walk around the outside of the cabin allowed her to see where an herb garden had once been. Left untended, the patch was a huge tangle, but she didn't fret over that small fact. One quick look assured her she'd have ample caraway, dill, rosemary, fennel, marjoram, basil, thyme, sage, and savory. For the time being, she took just enough to flavor the soup.

Satisfied that the attic now rated as habitable, Garnet dragged the empty mattress ticking up the ladder. Ethan followed her. "There's a pulley we can use to draw up the baskets of corn husks."

Fatigue pulled at her as she finished stuffing the mattress. Garnet watched Ethan scramble down the ladder, and then she gestured to her mouth, rubbed her tummy, and pointed toward the field.

"You want me to go fetch Father and Christopher for nuncheon?"

She nodded, so he dashed off.

≈

"Are you certain she wanted us to eat?" Christopher asked as he dried off his hands. He and his father exchanged dubious looks. Garnet hadn't taken any of the food from the fire. The keeping room smelled wonderful.

"We'll ready the table," Samuel decided. "Widow Wheelock might have stepped out a minute."

Hester set the table as he took the food from the fireplace. Garnet didn't show up. Samuel began to ladle the soup. The bowls were full, and Garnet's place still stayed vacant. "Hester, go to the privy and assure us that the widow fares well."

Hester giggled and ran out of the cabin. A few minutes later, she came back, but her face was sober. "The widow isn't there."

eight

Christopher rested his elbows on the table. "Do you think she ran away again, like she did last eve?"

"I cannot say. You children eat. I'll look for the widow. She's much too weak to go far." Samuel rose. He gave the pumpkin custard a longing look and sternly demanded, "Leave some of that for me. I've not had such a treat in a long while."

He went out and looked at the ground. Christopher's and Ethan's shoes left a definite imprint. Hester's tiny footprint stood out clearly, as did his own large ones. The other prints had to belong to Garnet. Samuel followed them, but they led to the springhouse. After following a few more tracks to the garden, he became more confused. He headed toward the stable to saddle up his horse, but he had no clue as to which direction Garnet had taken.

"Father! Come!" Hester ran up to him and threw her arms about his thighs.

He hugged her automatically. "What is it?"

"She's here! She was here all along!"

"Oh?"

Grabbing her father's hand, she put a finger to her lips and led him to the attic ladder. "Go see. She looks so peaceful, Father. We didn't have the heart to waken her."

Peaceful didn't begin to describe her. Garnet had fallen asleep on the boys' freshly aired and filled corn-husk mattress. Sam's brows furrowed at the sight of her in her rags. Why had

79

she changed back into such pathetic wear? He'd almost praised Garnet for looking handsome this morning—but 'twasn't fitting to do so. He'd gladly praise her cooking and how she treated his children, but a man oughtn't make personal statements if he didn't intend to court a woman. Nonetheless, he'd instruct her to wear Naomi's clothing hereafter.

Samuel took a blanket and covered her. She burrowed into the pillow. The action dislodged her cap, causing her glorious hair to spill freely across the bed. His fingers absently threaded through her mane, and he smiled softly. She'd kept her word, at least in part. She'd worked 'til midday, then rested. The smudge on her cheek told him that she wasn't yet ready to quit her labors.

Sam looked about the attic and caught his breath. It looked as it ought to—which was, sadly enough, something it never did anymore. Nary a speck of dirt, a web, or a stray feather could be seen. Indeed, the loft smelled fresh, and the boys' few possessions hung neatly on pegs. A woman's touch made a difference. He descended the ladder and went in to eat the soup. It tasted excellent, but the pumpkin custard truly got his attention.

"I'm thinking I'm glad we grew lots of pumpkins this year," Ethan declared with relish.

"You'd best see to weeding the garden," Samuel admonished his son as he served a goodly bit of custard onto his plate. The aroma of it made his mouth water. "After the garden is done, you and Christopher are to gather up the crockery and jars. Hester, you help them wash and dry all of them. We'll be needing to put by all of the vegetables and apples."

Ethan stared at his father's plate. His eyes shone with greed. "Might I have a little more custard ere I finish my labors?"

Samuel took a taste. "It is enough to tempt a body, isn't it?" He grinned as all three children nodded enthusiastically. "I confess the same weakness, but the widow will see no reward for her labors if we all have more. Be satisfied with your first helping—she will share the remainder at supper with us. It will be good for her to witness your thankful smiles."

After lunch, Sam went back to plowing the field. He'd cautioned the children to allow the widow to sleep. She'd accomplished far more than he thought possible and clearly worn herself out with the effort.

This morning, he'd decided the time had come for him to move up with the boys. Witnessing how weak Widow Wheelock was made him reconsider. Tomorrow, Ruth Morton would come over and they'd preserve apples. Even with Ruth's help and her daughter's assistance, such labor would still wear out the widow. Garnet would need a full day afterward to recover. Only she wouldn't rest. After the way she bargained to work half of today, Samuel knew she wouldn't be guilty of sloth.

Sunday. He nodded to himself. It seemed appropriate for him to move his bed on the day of rest. They'd go to worship this week. Missing church last week on account of Garnet's fever couldn't be helped. But this Sunday, after the service, he could tote the mattress from the trundle up to the chamber he'd share with his sons.

The breeze carried Hester's laughter. Sam delighted in it. "Lord, You've been faithful. I called upon Your name and asked You to bring my daughter home to me. You prepared a way and have mercifully increased the blessings so my sons will know the gentleness of a woman's care. I would never have imagined my prayers would be answered in this manner, but Your wisdom and mercy abound."

He plowed two more furrows, turning the stubble into the rich soil and praising God for His provision. Sam paused at the end of the field and wiped his brow with his sleeve. As he turned, his eyes narrowed.

"Samuel Walsh." A tall, sallow-faced man approached and nodded curtly.

"Erasmus Ryder." Sam wondered at the arrival of Dorcas's husband. The man had no reason to cease his labor early and come calling. "I trust all is well with you."

"We fare well enough. My goodwife tells me she's running out of wool."

The purpose of the visit fell into place. In years past, Dorcas and Erasmus claimed the shearing as payment for keeping Hester. As Sam's flock increased, Dorcas claimed that Hester was growing and it took more to keep her; thus the Ryders still took all of the shearing. Dorcas was known for her fine weaving, and the skill proved to be lucrative for her. Sam knew full well that even taking Dorcas's time and skill into account, the profit she made off his sheep's fleeces paid several times over what it cost for them to feed Hester. Since Hester wore hand-me-downs from Mary Morton, Dorcas hadn't had to clothe her. Nonetheless, creating ill will when his daughter lived under the Ryders' roof would be foolish indeed.

Only Hester no longer lived there. Samuel stood in silence, waiting for Erasmus to make him an offer on the wool.

Erasmus folded his arms across his chest. " 'Tis round the time you fall-shear your sheep."

"Indeed. But plenty wants doing. I'll get to it anon."

"Dorcas has need of the fleeces soon." Erasmus cast a look

toward the house, then added, "And you owe it to us."

Irritated by that comment, Samuel widened his stance. "The day Hester went to abide under your roof, you took the spring shearing. Dorcas has received the entirety of my fleeces in advance twice each year for the seasons to follow. The only indebtedness I hold is of gratitude."

"You would cheat us?"

"I'm an honorable man." Sam stared him in the eyes. "I gave over all of my wool in the years Hester lived beneath your roof. You've often boasted about how much Dorcas's cloth brings in. I've met my obligations fairly."

Erasmus glowered at him. "Best you reconsider. Taxes and tithe will come due."

"I cannot deny that is true."

"You'll need my tobacco. You cannot pay in wheat or corn. Nothing but Virginia tobacco is accepted, and you have none."

The exultant tone grated on Sam's nerves. He chose not to raise tobacco. It depleted the soil, and he considered smoking of the plant to be a distasteful habit. Nonetheless, he refused to be coerced. He wrapped his hands about the handle of the plow and shrugged. "I've always paid you full-market value for the tobacco required for my taxes and tithes. Thomas Brooks is a good friend to me, and he also grows tobacco."

"This is no way to treat family," Erasmus growled.

"I agree. Had you made me an offer on the fleeces, I would have struck a deal with you—a deal which took into account that Dorcas is my children's aunt. As it is, you tried to make an unjust claim."

Chin jutting forward, Erasmus rasped, "Reconsider. Once I walk away, I'll not deal with you again."

"I hold no agreement with you about buying your tobacco. You're welcome to sell it to any buyer, just as I am free to make arrangements with another grower. Indeed, Brooks has expressed how eager he'd be to have some of my cornmeal."

"You'll regret this, Samuel Walsh."

"Begone, Erasmus. I'll pretend this conversation never occurred."

"Remember it." The lanky man shook his finger at Sam. "Remember it well. You'll live to rue the day you crossed me."

nine

The scent of apples still filled the keeping room. Scores and scores of apple rings dried on pegs and strings all about the cabin. Apple peels steamed dry in shallow trays near the fire, and two crocks full of applesauce lined the wall near the table. A barrel with straw-packed apples sat in the springhouse.

Garnet stood in the doorway and waved good-bye to Ruth and Mary Morton. Hester slipped her sticky little hand into Garnet's. "Come back again soon. Widow Wheelock and me—we had fun."

" 'Twas a good day," Mary said. "But school starts again in a week."

Hester let out a little squeal. "I'm to go to school this year! Please, let's work together next week so we get everything done first!"

"I'm sure we will, Hester." Ruth waved. "We'll see you at worship on the morrow!"

The next two Sundays, Garnet enjoyed fine sermons. If only she could raise her voice with the congregation, though. When they sang hymns, she longed to join along.

A couple of weeks flew past. While the children were at school, Garnet tended a variety of chores and sometimes met with Ruth so they could work together. Garnet found contentment in her new life.

The next Saturday evening, Samuel watched as she

exchanged the water she'd soaked beans in all day. "Ruth must have told you about our custom of eating baked beans on Sunday."

Garnet added molasses and a little salt pork as she nodded. Tomorrow's meals would be curds and whey, baked beans, and pumpkin custard—all prepared with a minimum of labor tonight. She placed the bean pot in a spot she'd chosen. By setting the pot of beans near the fire all night, they'd be ready to eat on the morrow and relieve her from cooking on the Lord's day of rest.

Pumpkins were odd squashes, but Ruth Morton had shown her countless ways to use them one morning while the children were all at school. Rings of pumpkin now took the place of the apples on the drying pegs and strings all about the keeping room, and Garnet pulled a pan full of roasted seeds from the fire. Garnet slid the pumpkin seeds into a bowl she'd set on the table.

"The meals you make are toothsome, and you've been quick to learn how to prepare and preserve the foods specific to the colonies," Master Walsh praised. "You seem to enjoy cooking. What other things do you take pleasure in?"

She didn't have to pause to think. Garnet wheeled her finger vertically in the air, then pantomimed knitting.

"Spinning and knitting?" Master Walsh bolted to his feet. "Come with me, Widow Wheelock."

Perplexed, Garnet followed him out to the barn.

Master Walsh led her to the far corner of the structure and grabbed a hoe. He swung it in the air to banish thick cobwebs. "There."

Garnet leaned forward and clapped her hands for joy upon seeing a dust-covered spinning wheel. It was a smallish one made for spinning both flax and wool. She immediately thought about the sheep whose fleeces were heavy and of the small patch of flax.

"No doubt, it requires cleaning and the works are in wont of oiling, but we can see to that. Where's. . .there!" He located a tiny chest, blew the dirt and straw from the lid, and handed it to Garnet. "Carry that back to the house. I'll bring the spinning wheel."

While he painstakingly disassembled the spinning wheel over by the hearth, Garnet gathered rags. "Once I clean this and oil the wheel axle, it ought to serve well." Sam tested the leathers holding the bobbin and flyer. "The maidens are straight, and the mother-of-all is in fine condition."

She paused and watched as he deftly removed the flywheel. The firelight illuminated the beautifully turned spokes.

Sam laid the wheel on the table. "Flat as can be—I worried it might have grown warped. . . . The drive band is filthy. Can it be washed?"

Garnet inspected the dirty linen strip and nodded. Washing might alter its length, but she'd be able to adjust the tension to account for that.

"I'll set to work on this whilst you take stock of what's in the chest. If something is missing, we'll need to replace it ere the weather turns."

Garnet opened the chest. A pair of sewing needles, a paper of pins, and a daintily painted porcelain thimble rested in a small wood tray, which she removed. Three sets of knitting needles lay there along with a half-dozen balls of yarn. Then Garnet's heart leaped. A recorder rested in the bottom. Hands shaking, she drew out the instrument and offered it to her master.

He shook his head. "I put it out in the barn for good cause.

Neither Christopher nor I could coax any pleasant sounds from it. Are you able to play?"

Rubbing it on her sleeve, Garnet tried to decide what to play. After blowing through the recorder, she took a deep breath and started playing.

Master Walsh perked up, and the children all rushed in. After she finished the piece, he chortled with glee. " 'Butter'd Peas' is one of Ethan's favorite tunes!"

Christopher poked his brother in the side. "One of his favorite dishes, too."

"Will you teach me how?" Hester reached over and touched the instrument.

"Father, I used to have a whistle." Ethan scanned the keeping room. "Where is it?"

"A flageolet," Master Walsh remembered. "I'll have to think on where it went."

Ethan smiled up at his father. "I'll clean the spinning wheel while you look."

"Mind you clean every last nook and cranny. Any dust will spoil the yarn Widow Wheelock will spin." He handed the rag to his son and turned his attention back on Garnet. "We'd appreciate a few more tunes, Widow Wheelock."

Garnet thought for a moment, then raised the recorder and played "Childgrove." "Argeers" followed thereafter.

Christopher took up another rag and helped his brother. "Please don't stop," he pled.

Garnet looked to her master. He'd been wandering around, looking for the flageolet in vain. "I confess, I cannot recall where I put it. You've scoured every corner of the house, Widow Wheelock. Have you not seen it?"

She shook her head.

"What does it look like?" Hester tossed one of her plaits over her shoulder.

"It's smaller than the recorder Widow Wheelock is playing." Christopher scrunched his nose. "Wasn't it white?"

"No, it was pearwood." Furrows plowed across his father's brow. "The holes were brass."

"Is it a lot smaller?" Hester held her hands out so they were only six inches apart.

Christopher scrubbed one of the spinning wheel's spokes. "That's far too small."

"Two of the sections are that size, Hester." Sam stared at the fire. "The third is about the size of my thumb."

"I think I know where it is!" Hester scrambled to the far side of the keeping room and climbed onto the table.

"Hester!"

"Here, Father! See?" She stood on tiptoe and touched what looked like pegs. "I thought they looked funny when we took down the apple rings and put up the pumpkin rings."

"Now, I remember. Ethan dropped his whistle in the trough, so I put it up to dry." Samuel Walsh stalked over and pulled his daughter off the table. " 'Twas not mannerly of you to climb on this. Wipe it down and give Widow Wheelock an apology."

Garnet scarcely believed her ears. The master of the house ordered his daughter to apologize to her?

Hester approached Garnet and barely managed to bob a curtsy ere she burst into tears. "I f–f–forgot my–myself. I'm s–s–sorry."

Garnet set aside the recorder and opened her arms wide. Hester burrowed in close and clung tight as Garnet rocked her. When her storm of tears abated, she whispered, "Please don't be wroth with me!"

Garnet kissed her brow and smoothed her hand up and down the child's back.

"Widow Wheelock is a kind woman." Master Walsh dabbed tears from his daughter's cheeks with the edge of his shirt. "She labors hard. Be sure you don't cause her additional work."

"Yes, Father." Hester wound her arms around Garnet's neck and gave her a fierce hug. "I'm so glad you're here. I'm so glad I'm here."

"Well and good. Now see to the task." Master Walsh relocated the drying pumpkin rings to other pegs, puffed air through each of the pieces of the flageolet, and put them together while his daughter wiped off the table.

"I'd be pleased to hear another tune," Ethan said.

"And you will—tomorrow." Master Walsh smiled. "Thomas Brooks is taking his viol to worship tomorrow. Think how lovely 'twill be for Widow Wheelock to accompany him on the recorder or flageolet."

❧

Indeed, Garnet took both instruments to church the next day. She and Goodman Brooks played accompaniment as the congregation sang Isaac Watts's "O God, Our Help in Ages Past." Gerhardt's "Put Thou Thy Trust in God" came next. Though she couldn't sing the lyrics, Garnet thought of the words as she played. They suited her situation so clearly. She'd been reduced to nothingness; but God's strength sustained her, and He'd answered her prayers by placing her in the Walsh home.

> Put thou thy trust in God,
>   In duty's path go on;

Walk in His strength with faith and hope,
So shall thy work be done.

Lord, I put my trust in You. Though all I owned, and was, were stripped from me, You have been my stronghold. You heard my prayers and placed me in the Walsh home. I give You my thanks.

When the music ended, Garnet slipped onto the end of the Walsh bench. The preacher set his Bible on the pulpit. "Before I pray, the schoolmaster is suffering quinsy. As a result, he cannot teach for the next few days. Word will be sent out when school is to resume." The reverend prayed, then read from the third chapter of Proverbs. " 'Let not mercy and truth forsake thee. . . .' "

Garnet cast a quick look at her master. *He did just that—he's shown me great mercy.*

" 'Trust in the Lord with all thine heart; and lean not unto thine own understanding. In all thy ways acknowledge him, and he shall direct thy paths.' "

I don't understand all that has happened to me, but, Lord, You have a purpose. I trust in You.

After the service, Goodman Brooks called across the churchyard to them, "Hold a moment!"

"If you intend to talk about music, I'm sending Ruth to be part of the discussion," Falcon Morton announced. "There's nothing sweeter than the sound of her playing her dulcimore."

"Come then, Goodwife Morton." Goodman Brooks still held his viola de gamba as he approached. He then beckoned another man. "And you, Alex Smith. No one plays a fiddle more pleasingly than you." Ruth and Goodman Smith came over.

Another woman scurried up, as well, but something about how Samuel drew Hester close to his side struck Garnet as odd. He nodded politely. "Goodwife Ryder."

"Aunt Dorcas," all three of the Walsh children greeted in unison.

Instead of returning the pleasantry, the woman stuck out her hand, palm upward, toward Garnet. "That recorder was my sister's. By all rights, it should be mine now."

"No, it shouldn't." Master Walsh stepped up to Garnet's side.

Goodman Brooks shook his head, and in an excessively patient tone said, "Goodwife Ryder, all a wife owns belongs to her husband."

"Naomi owned her recorder ere she married." Dorcas tilted her head defiantly.

"Yes, she did," Smith agreed. "But upon marriage, two become one."

"Surely grief made you overlook that important truth," Ruth said in a kindly tone. "I recall you once played a cittern—and handily. It would be merry to add yet a different instrument to the group."

"Indeed. We'd have a quintet." Garnet jumped at the sound of the preacher's voice. He'd come over and now gave Dorcas a conciliatory smile. "I'm sure once you reflect upon it that you'll not begrudge Widow Wheelock playing the recorder. 'Tis a blessing for her to be able to give sound, if not voice, in worship."

Most of the congregation milled around; clearly they were eavesdropping.

A man stood behind Dorcas and rested his hands upon her shoulders. Hatred twisted his features as he looked first at

Samuel, then at Garnet. "You cannot blame my wife. Walsh has given Naomi's clothing to his servant. My wife looks upon her, and her grief is renewed. For that woman to stand before the congregation and play Naomi's recorder is more hypocrisy than is to be borne. Know this, Parson: They sleep beneath the same roof. Furthermore, whilst the children are at school, Walsh and this woman are alone."

ten

"Your implication is vile." Samuel stared straight back at Erasmus Ryder. "The widow and my daughter sleep in the keeping room; I sleep in the second story with my sons."

"There, then." Reverend Clark nodded his head. "Samuel Walsh is a man of sterling character. We've his word that naught is awry."

"If it troubles you to see Naomi's clothing. . ." Ruth Morton patted Dorcas's hand. "Mayhap you ought to give her some of the fine cloth you weave. I'll help her sew a new set of overclothes— though she probably needs no assistance. Christopher wears the shirt she stitched for him, and little Hester is charming as a chickadee in the new bodice the widow made from the scraps of her very own clothes. Still, if it grieves you to witness another wearing the clothing Naomi once wore, this arrangement will allow you to trade for your sister's garments."

"All of my cloth is spoken for. I cannot renege."

"I have no patience for this." Sam scowled. Dorcas would find fault in any bargain or solution. Garnet already labored long and hard. He couldn't imagine making her sew another set of clothing merely because Dorcas indulged in pettiness and greed. "Children wear clothing handed down because 'tis sensible. When someone perishes, other than the attire in which they are buried, any other garments go to others who can make use of it. So I've done, and no one should find fault in it."

"You buried my sister in nothing more than a blanket!"

Samuel stood in silence. He didn't need to defend himself or his actions.

"Father?" Christopher gave him a beseeching look.

I was wrong. Though I needn't defend myself, I cannot allow my children to believe I dishonored their mother.

Falcon cleared his throat. "My goodwife and I were present at the time. Given the circumstances, Naomi—"

"Given the circumstances?" Dorcas gave Falcon a withering look.

"Your mother caught fire whilst preparing breakfast," Samuel said softly.

A slight gasp escaped Garnet. She immediately took Ethan and Hester by their hands and led them off.

"I knew she got burned." Christopher still looked confused.

"I wrapped your mother in a blanket to put out the flames." Samuel wished his son didn't have to hear this. He chose his words carefully. "Her burns were severe. The very morning of the accident, she went to her Maker."

"In nothing," Dorcas snapped, "more than a burned nightdress and a blanket."

"Her pain was great, Christopher," Ruth said. "I sat with your father at her bedside for half the morning until she slipped away. We buried Naomi gently. Dressed as she was in her nightdress and the quilt she favored, she looked peaceful. She'd gone on to her eternal rest."

Christopher nodded slowly. "Thank you, Goodwife Morton, for being a friend in my mother's time of trouble. Aunt Dorcas? Surely my mother would be gladdened that someone in need received her clothes."

Reverend Clark smiled. "Well said, lad. A godly woman's

heart is full of charity."

Unwilling to allow the Ryders any further opportunity to upset his son or promulgate falsehoods, Sam said, "I bid you all good day."

"Good day," the others said—all save the Ryders who turned and walked away.

Falcon said, "Christopher, since there's to be no school on the morrow, I plan to send Aaron to chip out salt blocks in the morn. If perchance your father needs more, my son would be glad of your company and help."

"Father?"

Resting his hand on his son's shoulder, Sam said, "I'll send Christopher over with the wagon. He recently spotted a salt vein."

"If the boys bring me salt, as well, I'd be willing to spend the morrow on a trip to the coast." Brooks grinned. "A good-sized sturgeon would feed us all many a meal."

"The last time he did so, Reverend, the fish he hauled back was enormous." Ruth slipped her hand into Falcon's. "You'll have to come for supper."

"Aaron and I will fetch even more salt." Christopher's eyes glittered. "Reverend Clark, you weren't here yet. The last time Goodman Brooks brought back a sturgeon, he found it necessary to behead the creature and chop off the tail just to fit the body diagonally in his wagon!"

"I'd be pleased to have such a fine meal." Reverend Clark grimaced. "The best that can be said of my cooking is that 'tis warm."

"There's always a place at our table for you," Ruth said.

"The same can be said for my household." Sam and Christopher walked back toward the wagon. On the way to church, Garnet had shared the seat with Samuel. Now, she'd climbed into the back with Ethan and Hester—due, no doubt, to Erasmus's base accusation. Sam tamped down the urge to order her onto the seat. After nuncheon, he'd speak with her privately.

"You said—" Chris's voice cracked, and he coughed into his hand to cover the embarrassment. "You said I'd drive the wagon on the morrow."

"Indeed." Sam clapped his son on the back. "In fact, you'll drive us home today."

Wisdom dictated he sit beside his son on the bench. Still, Sam didn't want to have everyone in the churchyard believe he allowed Ryder's crudity to leave any taint. He stood by the side of the wagon and squinted at Hester's bodice. "If my estimate is correct, you could take the lacing from that and use it to play cat's cradle on the trip home."

"Widow Wheelock taught me how to play that." Hester immediately started to pull the lace free.

"She's teaching us many things," Ethan hastened to say.

Christopher climbed up onto the seat. "I'll be sure to bring home sufficient salt for you, Widow Wheelock. With all the pickling and salting and drying you've been doing, you'll need more."

Garnet smiled at Chris.

Sam thought of all the herbs, vegetables, and fruits she'd been preserving and drying. "Thanks to her industry, your belly won't just be warm and full this winter. 'Twill be tasty fare we enjoy."

Ann Stamsfield's giggles filled the air as her husband drove by them. She called back, "Anything would have to be an improvement, Goodman Walsh!"

Upon taking his first bite at nuncheon, Christopher looked across the table. "Widow Wheelock, Goodwife Stamsfield teased Father that anything would be better than his cooking. Since you've come, the stirabout in the morning is never burned, and I've not had a single bellyache."

Samuel waggled his spoon at his son. "Your cooking was no better. For mercy's sake, Widow Wheelock, please be sure to teach Hester how to make such fine food. One of these days when a man takes her to wife, he will be thankful for the kindness."

"I'm thankful now." Ethan eyed the pumpkin. "Especially for that custard."

"Eat the rest of your nuncheon, son. No sweet until you've finished what's already on your plate."

Four times in the past two weeks, Garnet had made pumpkin custard. Ruth had also shown her how to make pumpkin muffins and pumpkin pie. While many of the pumpkins sat out in the field curing, those without a stem attached wouldn't keep well. On the day Ruth and Garnet made soap, Ruth taught her to cut those pumpkins into rings to dry.

"Father," Hester swallowed a bite, "is it work to go on a walk and gather?"

"It would depend on what you gather and why you took the walk. If your brother went on a walk to set snares and collect the creatures they'd captured, that would be work. If you went for a stroll and found a patch of flowers that made you happy, then gathering them to share God's beauty on our table would be fine."

"Any plant out there, the widow can find a use for. Many uses. On Sundays, if she takes me for a stroll and the flowers are pretty on the table that day and she can use them the next day, is that work?"

"Each person must examine his own heart and submit to the Lord. It isn't for me to judge what another feels is acceptable to God. I must live as He gives me light. Widow Wheelock has shown a love for the Lord and great kindness. I trust she would act in accordance with what she knows in her heart to be right."

In keeping with it being the day of rest, neither Garnet nor he could busy themselves with ordinary chores. After they'd enjoyed the custard, Sam rose. "Today's fair, but it won't be long ere we deal with the cold. Why don't we all take a stroll to the stream? You children may wade."

His children hopped up and bolted out the door.

Sam picked up the slate. "Come, Widow Wheelock. Christopher swims like a fish, and Ethan manages to paddle around well enough to enjoy himself, but I worry for Hester."

Garnet made a shooing motion with her hands.

"Come along with you." Sam used the tone and expression he used when his sons bordered on being stubborn. Garnet's cheeks flushed, and she bowed her head—but she started toward the door. Samuel followed close on her heels, then shut the door behind them. "There's a spot I've always taken the boys to. 'Tis wider and more shallow than where we fetch the water by the house, so 'tis a better place to allow them to frolic. Ethan and Hester can enjoy themselves quite safely. This way."

Reaching the stream took no time at all, but Samuel led her almost fifty yards farther downstream. He sat on a log he'd placed there long ago and patted the spot beside him. "We can watch the children from here."

Garnet smiled at the sight of Ethan kicking water at Christopher. She started toward the stream, but Samuel halted her. "Sit. We need to talk."

Wariness painted her features. Slowly, she sat on the log—almost a yard away.

"Erasmus Ryder holds a grudge against me. In his anger, he insinuated you and I have. . .sinned."

The widow's cheeks blazed; then suddenly the color drained away, and her lower lip quivered ever so slightly before she bit it. Her hand shook as she reached for the slate. Slowly, she formed the letters and gave it back to him. *I will leaf.*

"No! Absolutely not."

The saddest smile he'd ever seen lifted the corners of her mouth as her head bobbed up and down.

"There's no reason at all for you to leave and every reason to stay. You've made my house a home, and because of your presence, Hester is with us. I've been desperate to bring her home. After seeing how Dorcas and Erasmus behave, surely you wouldn't want her to return to them."

Garnet looked horrified at the thought.

"As you heard Dorcas say, she and my wife were sisters. The truth is a bitter one: I was young, foolish, and lonely. In a matter of one slim week, I met and married Naomi. Eight years we were wed, and not a single day passed without strife. Naomi was the mother of my children, and I will not speak against her. Suffice it to say, I will never again marry."

That same sad smile crossed her features as she tapped her breastbone and shook her head.

"You are a widow and were sold to cover your husband's debts. Are you telling me 'twas not a happy union?" Her expression was more eloquent than words. "It grieves me to know your marriage brought you no contentment. If you remain, you won't have to marry just to keep a roof over your head and food in you."

Her eyes fluttered shut, and she let out a silent exhalation, then looked at him. Gratitude gleamed in her eyes, turning them silver. Her lips moved, forming *Thank you.*

"Before you thank me, I would be honest with you." He rubbed his sweaty palms on the knees of his worn breeches. "There's no doubt in my mind: Erasmus will be a thorn in our sides. He tried to sully your virtue and damage my reputation. Alas, I expect him to persist."

Her lips twisted into a wry smile, and she shrugged.

Glad that she had the courage to put up with the bedeviling they'd inevitably suffer from the Ryders, Sam dared to ask what he'd hoped for since the day he bought her. "I granted you your freedom, and so you are free; yet I ask you now, Garnet Wheelock, to give me your promise to remain here as a valued member of my family."

She pressed her hands together.

"Would you have me pray, or are you asking for time to pray, yourself?"

She scooted off the log and cast a look at the distance.

"Aye. Go and talk with the Lord. It is fitting to seek His wisdom in all things." Garnet disappeared behind a grove of trees, and Samuel turned his attention on the children. Ethan handed Hester a little boat he'd made from a bit of bark and a leaf. She squealed with joy and set it in the water. As it started to float, she wrapped her arms around Ethan's waist and hugged him. By the time she looked back, her boat had drifted out of reach. She let out a cry and started to go after it. For an instant, Samuel started to rise.

Christopher grabbed Hester by the waist and twirled her back onto dry land. "Let's go make more!"

Seeing Christopher attend Hester allowed Sam to sit back down. Garnet showed wisdom in seeking the Lord's will. Sam rubbed his hands on his knees again. *I'm never anxious, yet I'm even more nervous than when I asked Naomi to wed me. Naomi was a stranger to me; the widow abides beneath my roof and has proven to be of excellent character. She is kind beyond telling and holds great affection for the children. Surely that will sway her to make this commitment.*

But what if she doesn't?

The Eighty-fourth Psalm ran through his mind, and he recited it aloud. " 'For the Lord God is a sun and shield: the Lord will give grace and glory: no good thing will he withhold from them that walk uprightly. O Lord of hosts, blessed is the man that trusteth in thee.' Father of light, You have blessed me richly. I place my trust in You. If it be Your will, press upon the widow's heart how desperately we need her. Be my family's shield against Erasmus's plots. Safeguard us and be the sunlight that illuminates the path we are to follow. In Christ Jesus' name. Amen."

"Father!" Hester beckoned him. "Come make boats with us!"

Sam gathered several leaves, twigs, and bits of bark, then went and sat at the edge of the stream. Hester plopped into his lap, and Sam enveloped her in his arms. Hester didn't stay long. She hopped up and set the next boat a-sail. Pleasure rippled through Sam as he watched his children frolic. Finally, he stood. "It's time we went home."

Garnet sat over on the log. One look at her expression, and Sam's heart fell.

eleven

I promise. Garnet had written the words because deep in her heart she knew God wouldn't have brought her across the ocean and put her through all of her trials without having a purpose. During her prayer, a sense of certainty filled her that His intent was to allow her the joy of children and a family without ever having to wed again. In the three weeks she'd been with the Walshes, she'd been provided for and treated with kindness and respect. Even so, Garnet didn't believe in making promises lightly. Writing those two words committed her, and she felt the gravity of her vow as she waited for Master Walsh.

"Look!" Hester pointed. "Widow Wheelock wrote us a message! What does it say?"

Ethan ran ahead, but Garnet kept her gaze on Master Walsh. "I promise," Ethan read aloud, and relief transformed his father's features.

"What do you promise, Widow Wheelock?" Christopher's brows furrowed, momentarily making him look exactly as his father had on other occasions.

"I asked her to give us her word that she would remain here." Joy radiated from Samuel, and he scooped Hester into his arms. "Because of your promise and generous spirit, Garnet, my family is together, and my daughter will learn how to keep a happy home. We are all beholden to you for all you have done and will do."

"And I'll help you." Hester hooked one arm around his neck and twisted toward Garnet. "We can garden and cook, and whilst you spin, I can card wool. Aunt Dorcas set me to that task every day."

"That's a fine plan." Samuel tickled Hester's tummy. "I suppose I ought to shear the sheep on the morrow, then."

"But I was to go get salt," Christopher said.

"And so you will. I'll accompany you to the Mortons', and after Falcon and I shear his sheep, we'll come here and do ours. I'm sure Goodwife Morton would be amenable to sharing a chore with Widow Wheelock. You and Aaron bring the salt here, and we'll all preserve the fish together."

Garnet wiped the slate and wrote as quickly as she could, *Ruth asked preecher to supper.*

"Yes, she did." Samuel shrugged. "Henry, John, and Peter Morton could give the message to the reverend, then walk over here to fetch Ethan. Ethan, you may use the wheelbarrow so you boys can go gather beechnuts, butternuts, walnuts, and acorns. Until the Morton boys arrive, I want you and Hester to go pick the last of the beans and peas."

They all walked back to the house. Ethan lifted the recorder from the table and handed it to Garnet. "Would you please play a tune?"

Garnet thought a moment, then began to play the simple notes.

Samuel Walsh sat by the hearth and cuddled his daughter close as he began to sing, " 'Praise God, from whom all blessings flow. . . .' " The fierce tenderness of his hold and the sincerity of his voice touched Garnet deeply.

The next day, Garnet heard Master Walsh singing that same hymn as he set out toward the Mortons'. Garnet set to work at once. She wanted to accomplish several tasks ere Ruth arrived.

Just past midmorning, Ruth arrived. She barely scrambled down from her wagon ere she dashed off and purged her stomach.

Garnet dampened a rag, knelt beside her, and blotted her friend's face.

"Don't fret over me. I'm not sickening." Ruth managed a wan smile. "I told Falcon this morn that we're to be blessed with another child. The first months, my stomach puts up a fight."

Empathy flooded Garnet. She'd always been hale, but when her husband had gambled away all they owned, hunger drove her to eat food that must have been spoiled. She hadn't recovered from that ere they put her aboard the ship and seasickness plagued her.

Ruth took the rag and passed it over her own face. "Don't look so worried, Garnet. The time I carried Mary, I was sickest of all. Since the nausea is bad again this time, I'm hoping the babe will be a girl."

Fleetingly running her hand across Ruth's tummy, Garnet frowned. She couldn't feel so much as a tiny hint of a babe.

"No, I won't show for a few months yet. By then, the sickness will cease. It only lasts the first few months."

Garnet rose and helped Ruth stand.

"Samuel made me promise that you'd nap after nuncheon." Ruth let out a small laugh. "In truth, 'twas a promise easily made. Whene'er I'm carrying, fatigue nigh unto overwhelms me at midday."

Staring at Ruth, Garnet couldn't respond.

"I won't feel quite so guilty resting since you will, too. Garnet? Garnet!"

Everything inside her started shaking, and no matter how hard she tried, Garnet couldn't draw a breath.

"Here. Come here now." Ruth tugged her over a few yards and leaned her against the split rail fence.

"Mama? I brought you water." Mary held out the dipper.

"Nicely done." Ruth took it. "Take Hubert and Hester with you and go a-gathering. We'll need herbs aplenty when the fish arrives."

"Is the widow ailing again, Mama? She's wan as can be."

"Off with you, Mary. Do my bidding." Ruth pressed the dipper to Garnet's mouth. "Sip this. We must talk."

Having carried many children, Ruth asked some piercing questions and pressed one of Garnet's hands between her own. "You carry a life within you. You're shocked, but things will work out. By my reckoning, you have almost five months to go—that's time aplenty for you to get used to the fact and prepare."

Misery swamped Garnet. As a little girl, she'd dreamed of her future. She'd marry a man who cared for her, and they'd have babes to cradle. Her dreams came to naught but nightmares. Her husband had given her nothing but heartache and a babe he'd not be around to support.

And what will Samuel Walsh say? Surely, when he asked me to stay, he didn't anticipate I'd have a child.

The rest of the morning passed in a blur. Accustomed to marshaling her sizable family, Ruth took over and organized chores for the children and kept Garnet busy.

"We finished faster than we expected."

Samuel's voice made Garnet spin around.

"I confess," he said as he put the spring-back shears on the table, " 'twas the thought of eating a tasty nuncheon that spurred Falcon and me to shear his flock so quickly."

"You'll have wool aplenty to spin this winter." Falcon gave his wife an affectionate pat.

"Father!" Henry burst through the doorway. "We just brought back our third wheelbarrow full of nuts!"

"Bring back a fourth; then you may eat." Ruth shooed him away and tugged on her husband's hand. "Come, Falcon." A moment later, Ruth shut the door, leaving Samuel and Garnet alone in the keeping room.

Samuel gave Garnet a quizzical look. "Ruth's behaving oddly. Do you suppose 'tis because she's increasing? Falcon told me they will be blessed with another child."

Slowly shaking her head, Garnet took up the slate. She bit her lip, gathered all of her courage, and wrote down a few words.

❧

I have babe to.

For a moment, Sam stared at the slate and felt a bolt of sheer anger. *I had everything planned. This will ruin it.* Sam tore his gaze from those stark words and looked at Garnet. "You're with child."

Eyes wide and glistening, she nodded and swiped away the first message.

I can't tell whether she's happy or devastated. The first noontime Ruth came to call, she inquired if this might be a possibility, yet I banished it from my mind. 'Twas foolish of me.

Garnet caught her lower lip between her teeth. Laboriously, she scribed, *You want me to lea—*

"Give me that." Sam yanked away the slate and set it on the mantel. Curling his hands around her upper arms, he pivoted. "Sit, Garnet."

She sank onto the bench and clenched her hands in her lap. Though he'd considered her already pale, all color bled from her face.

"Am I to take it that you've just realized your condition?"

Her head bobbed a jerky affirmative.

Naomi resented carrying our children. She made life miserable because she— He caught himself. *I cannot compare Garnet to her. Garnet is a different woman and has displayed nothing but a sweet temperament.*

"This changes nothing." As Sam voiced those words, resolve built within him. "No, it doesn't." He rested one knee on the bench and tilted her face up to his.

The cloudy tint to her eyes testified to her confusion and concern.

"Neither of us counted on this eventuality, but the Lord chose to quicken a life within you, and we bow to His wisdom." Though he spoke the truth, it sounded harsh. Sam couldn't honestly say this development pleased him, but the widow oughtn't be made to feel guilty. He cleared his throat. "Widow Wheelock, you promised to stay and help my children. I make that same promise in return. I will provide for your child as I would for my own."

Tears spilled down her cheeks.

Sam couldn't tell the cause of her tears—relief? grief? delight? But he had no right to ask such personal questions. Having the babe would strain her. She was not yet fully recovered from her ordeals. A thought shot through him. "Garnet, 'tis a difficult question I pose you, but I would know: In the time since your husband died, has any man forced himself upon you?"

She shook her head.

"So your husband sired the babe." Relief flooded Samuel. The Almighty had spared her that horrific burden. "You will continue to abide here, and we'll pray the Lord gives you succor in the months ahead."

Her narrow shoulders straightened. Garnet wiped away her tears, and determination painted her features. She took up the slate and wrote, *This changes no thing.*

The very words I spoke to her. Samuel nodded once with great emphasis. "This alters nothing whatsoever." In his mind, he agreed completely, but his heart called him a liar.

With all of the children at the table, nuncheon passed quickly and without any further discussion of the pregnancy. As soon as he finished his bowl of stew, Samuel rose. "We've sheep to shear."

Falcon stood. "And you have three more than I. We'll have them done by the time Brooks arrives with the fish."

Once they were out in the barn, Sam let out a heavy sigh. "Ruth told you?"

"Aye." Falcon said nothing more. They set to work, but instead of the jocularity they'd enjoyed that morn, the men remained silent. Finally finishing the last ewe, Falcon said, "Even with Brooks fetching the sturgeon, I need to replenish my smokehouse. What say you to us going hunting?"

"Venison would suit me."

"After that turkey you shot, Ruth's been after me to get a few."

"It made for good eating."

Falcon leaned back and studied Sam's face. "Left to your own devices, you or Christopher would have burned it o'er the fire. You might think to dwell on the improvements in your life now that the widow is here."

"The problem with sage advice is that 'tis easier to give than to live. Nonetheless, Hester is home. For that, I'll endure—"

Ruth cleared her throat loudly.

Sam wheeled around. Ruth wasn't alone. The shattered look on Garnet's face told him she'd heard his thoughtless words.

twelve

"The first shot downed that stag," Samuel Walsh said. "Widow Wheelock is the one who loaded my flintlock. Her red hair about the trigger reminded me so. She ought to take some credit for the fine venison we'll all be eating."

Garnet pretended she hadn't heard him. She'd rinsed the tripe thrice, making it suitable for casing sausage. Ruth and Mary both chopped the bits of meat left over after Sam and Falcon both butchered their bucks.

"I can tell you fattened your swine with milk and corn. 'Twill be tasty," Ruth said. "Are you sure you want to share the pork?"

Garnet nodded emphatically.

"You know venison sausage alone tastes gamey. The hog was of great size, and adding the pork to the sausage will improve it." Sam stared at the bucket of dill, fennel, onion, and garlic Garnet had washed, dried, and minced. "Adding Widow Wheelock's spices will make for an excellent flavor."

Garnet walked in the opposite direction and added more tansy to the steaming pots of water. The smell kept flies away from the butchering. If only there were a way to keep Master Walsh away. *He spoke his mind to a friend, and I heard the truth. Surely he cannot believe fulsome praise will make me forget the truth. I am here by his sufferance.*

Slaughtering a hog at the same time they dressed two deer made for a long, wearying day. Garnet appreciated Ruth's help, but even more, she needed her presence. Trying to do all of this alone with Master Walsh would have been impossibly awkward.

By the day's end, venison, sausage, and ham joined the fish hanging from crossbeams and pegs in the smokehouse. Garnet and Ruth boiled the tongues and fried the livers, and both families ate together. Afterward, Samuel went to the Mortons' so he could help suspend the meat in their smokehouse. Garnet fell asleep with thanksgiving—not only for the providence of plentiful food, but also for Samuel's temporary absence.

The next afternoon, Garnet inspected the meat and assured herself it was curing well. Nothing looked spoiled. She added another handful of hickory chips to the fire.

"It's hot in here." Hester wrinkled her nose. "It doesn't smell pretty like when you cook."

Garnet forced a smile and led the little girl from the smokehouse. While the children were at school in the mornings, Garnet strove to complete tasks too difficult for Hester. By keeping the simpler chores for when the little girl came home from school, she managed to make Hester feel both cherished and helpful. With the schoolmaster sick, Hester followed Garnet like a little shadow. Garnet loved her chatter and companionship. After Garnet latched the smokehouse door, they picked up their buckets and started toward the house.

"Ho, now. What have we here?" Reverend Clark dismounted and pointed toward Hester's pail.

Beaming, Hester swung her pail from side to side. "Widow Wheelock never walks out without returning with herbs for cooking and healing. The herb garden was a fright, but we've reclaimed it. She's teaching me plant lore."

"That's a fine thing." The parson scanned the yard and asked, "Where's your father?"

"On the other side of the barn, sir. He's scraping a deer hide." Hester popped up on tiptoe and added, "He shot a big buck."

"So I heard. Your brother Christopher also helped bag some fine turkeys. I was most grateful to receive one, as was your schoolmaster."

Hester threaded her small hand into Garnet's. "The widow and me—we've been busy. She's teaching me how to salt and pickle and cure all sorts of things. We spent yesterday making sausage. Did you know that adding pork to the venison makes for a better sausage?"

"Indeed."

Hester continued to chatter. "The smokehouse is full now."

"God be praised for His bounty." The parson looked at Garnet. "Widow Wheelock, mayhap you could accompany me to pay a call on Samuel Walsh. Hester, take the widow's bucket along with yours and go bind the herbs for drying. I'm sure Widow Wheelock will be pleased to come back to the keeping room and see how industrious you've been."

Unsure as to why the parson had come, Garnet accompanied him toward the barn. It would be fitting to welcome him to their nuncheon table, but she would leave that to Samuel. In the past two weeks, they'd accomplished much about the farm. They both labored diligently, but a strain existed between them.

Her shock about her maternal condition gave way to a mix of wonder and sadness. Though Garnet would never marry again, God had chosen to give her a child of her own. 'Twas a gift beyond imagining—but Samuel considered her babe an encumbrance. She'd vowed to remain here, and her word was her bond. Samuel promised to provide for the baby—more than Garnet could do on her own—but a child ought to be cherished, not just tolerated. Emotions and concerns bundled into a knot in her stomach. Just yestereve, Garnet decided her inability to speak had turned out to be a blessing in this situation.

"Samuel Walsh."

Sam looked up from the hide. "Reverend Clark. Welcome."

"So Ethan is of an age where he's helping with deer hide." The reverend smiled at Ethan. "You're on your way to manhood."

The sound of the axe made him turn to the side. "I see Christopher's chopping more firewood. A good thing, too. Winter's on its way."

Sam rose and wiped his hands on his thighs. "That's a fact. My winter wheat is already sown."

"The wind carries a decisive chill. Mayhap we ought to take Widow Wheelock into the barn, out of the cold."

Garnet tensed. Until now, she'd believed this to be a social visit. Clearly, it wasn't. The parson quite deftly had managed to ascertain where the children were, then asked Samuel and Garnet to come away from them for a private conversation.

As they entered the barn, the parson halted. "Is that a cheese ladder?"

"Aye. The widow's been making use of the overage of milk. As you said, the wind's stronger. She asked me to move the ladder inside so the cheese won't be tough. Widow Wheelock, when the reverend takes his leave, perchance could you allow him some cheese?"

Garnet nodded.

"You work together well." The parson looked from Garnet to Samuel and back again.

"The widow is unafraid of labor. She puts her hand to any task quite willingly."

Samuel's praise would mean far more if he didn't keep referring to me as "the widow." He does it a purpose, too. He means to remind me and all others that I am set apart from him.

"It is rumored that you are with child, Widow Wheelock."

She gave the parson a startled look.

"Word reached Goodwife Ryder. She's gathered a handful of others and approached me, saying Hester needs to be removed from this unwholesome place and returned to her care."

Samuel bristled. "Hester is staying here. Dorcas and Erasmus are angry at me and seek to cause strife."

"I supposed that might be so after the incident in the churchyard, but there is still the—" The parson shot a look at Garnet. "The other matter."

"The widow bears her husband's child." Sam's tone held a definite edge. "When the babe is born early next spring, 'twill be evident the gossipmongers were wrong in assuming I'm the sire."

"The Ryders wasted no time in spreading tales. Until spring comes and your point is proven, it would be best for Hester to—"

"No!" Sam's eyes burned with fury. "My daughter is not a pawn to be moved about in some game."

Reverend Clark picked some lint from his sleeve. The seemingly casual action didn't fool Garnet in the least. He looked at Samuel. "It defies the natural order of things for a woman to be alone—especially when she is with child. Four of the men in the congregation have reminded me of that fact and stated they are willing to wed the widow."

Clenching her teeth, Garnet shook her head.

Samuel's eyes narrowed. "Not a whit do I care for what others may say or wish. The widow has vowed to remain to assist my household, and I promised to provide for her and her child. The arrangement suits us."

The parson remained silent for a few minutes. "The Bible exhorts us to abstain from the very appearance of evil. The arrangement, which suits the two of you, sets a poor example for the children. The Lord Himself said it was not good for man to be alone and thus He created Eve. By keeping Widow Wheelock here, you rob some other man of the God-given need to be complete."

The parson's features pulled. "I confess, I hoped to answer the issue by way of the fact that the woman was bought; therefore, she is your indentured servant. When Goodman Brooks told me that you bought her as a bride and hold such papers, I lost the ability to justify your reason to keep a woman here without wedding her."

Samuel bristled yet again. "Thomas Brooks asked for her?"

"He did so out of mercy. Alan Cooper was boasting to him that he'd decided to place a claim on her. Thomas said if you'd not wed Widow Wheelock, he would."

A wave of revulsion washed over Garnet. She'd seen Alan Cooper at church. He stank of libation and leered at the women. Brooks had shown great kindness in trying to spare her such a match.

"You've backed me into a corner." Sam's face darkened. "The only way I'm to keep this woman here is to wed her. If I fail to do so, you'll remove Hester from my home?"

"I would not, but the council has the power to do so."

"Ryder is on the council." The muscle in Samuel's jaw spasmed.

"He is." Reverend Clark paused, then added, "The council is to meet regarding the matter tonight. I hoped to appeal to you ere it came to that."

"I stand by my word. I promised Hester she is home to stay, and I vowed to provide for the Wheelock child. If marriage is the only way for me to do so, then I have no choice. We will wed."

Garnet watched as the men shook hands. *Once again, I'm bartered in marriage. Samuel is bleak. He doesn't want me, yet he spoke for us both.*

"I'd normally conduct the marriage on Sunday after the sermon, but waiting is unwise."

"Ruth and Falcon can witness the marriage." Sam finally looked at Garnet. "I'll hitch the wagon whilst you gather my children."

My children. Before they'd discovered she was with child, Samuel always said "the children." Ever since, he'd referred to them as his—a potent reminder that she and her babe were outsiders.

She held out her left palm and walked two fingers across it.

"No. We'll ride." Impatience tainted his voice. "It's faster, and we'll get this over with at once."

Sam didn't say a word on the drive over to the Mortons'. It turned out that Falcon was at Thomas Brooks's. Ruth sent Aaron to go fetch him. Still, Sam remained utterly silent.

"Mary, you and Hester go gather some pretty flowers. A bride deserves beauty on her wedding day." Ruth tugged Garnet toward the house and called back over her shoulder,

"Let us know when the men arrive."

Ruth shut the door, then let out a mirthless laugh. "If I don't miss my guess, Sam didn't propose—he ordered."

Folding her arms across her chest, Garnet nodded.

Dipping a rag into water, Ruth said, "Falcon did the same with me. He later told me he wouldn't allow me a choice because he feared I'd refuse." She handed the soggy cloth to Garnet and urged her to freshen up. "I reminded Falcon that I could have spoken my denial when asked to speak the vows. Can you believe he'd not thought of that?"

Ruth barely paused to draw in a breath as she swiped the cap from Garnet's head and started to run a brush through her hair. "I'll bet Samuel hasn't thought of that, either. Then again, you can't speak. They'll allow you to nod your head. Hear me, Garnet. 'Twill be a sound union. Other than my Falcon, there's not a finer man in all of the colonies. You and your child could do no better.

"Mary came home from school yesternoon saying Erasmus Ryder was congratulating the Cooper man on finding a wife. Now I know why. I'm not sure whether it's a sin or not, but I'm relishing the fact that their scheme failed. No, now that I think of it, it can't be a sin. King David was a man after God's own heart, and he wrote many a psalm in which he delights in how the wicked are laid low."

She teased out a snarl and continued to brush Garnet's hair. "This marriage will protect you from such scheming men, and that is good. Better still, you and Samuel make a fine team. Yes, this marriage is right, no matter which way I look at it."

Lord, what am I to do? The day we learned I'm with child, Samuel changed. He said he'd endure anything to keep Hester home, and so he's being pushed into a marriage he resents. I don't want it, either. How are we to abide beneath the same roof in harmony?

❧

"Do you, Garnet Wheelock, give your consent to wed and freely enter into the covenant of holy matrimony?"

Clutching a handful of flowers, Garnet stood at Sam's side. For the first time, he realized she'd been herded into this, too. He'd been so desperate to shelter Hester that he'd been blind to the fact that Garnet was caught in the same trap. His blood boiled at the thought of Cooper trying to wed her. No woman ought be bound to such a sot.

Reverend Clark held *The Book of Common Prayer* and had already made opening comments concerning the church and holy matrimony. Never before had Sam paid any attention to the fact that the reverend always ascertained publicly if the bride and groom were willing.

The corners of Garnet's mouth tightened, and her shoulders rose with the deep breath she took.

Agree, Garnet. Though not pleased, I'm at least willing. He stared down at her, silently entreating her to grant approval for the ceremony to continue.

thirteen

The color of Garnet's eyes darkened to a pewter gray as her head dipped and rose in a nod—tiny as it was.

"Fine then," Reverend Clark responded. "Samuel, repeat after me. 'I, Samuel, take thee, Garnet, to my wedded wife. . . .'"

Samuel not only repeated the words but carried on without any prompting, "to have and to hold from this day forward, for better for worse, for richer for poorer, in sickness and in health, to love and to cherish, till death do us part, according to God's holy ordinance; and thereto I plight thee my troth."

Reverend Clark turned to Garnet. "As you cannot repeat after me, place your hand upon Samuel's. I'll place my hand atop yours, and with each phrase, you can signal your vow by squeezing."

Small calluses roughened the tips of her fingers and her palm. Garnet was no stranger to hard work, yet her hand felt impossibly small compared to his. Sam noted that her hand remained steady. She squeezed with the reading of each phrase until Reverend Clark read, "to love and to cherish."

Sam had rushed through his recitation, stating the words by rote. With each phrase requiring Garnet's attention, Sam felt the full impact of the vows. Softly, he murmured, " 'Tis sufficient that we care for each other in Christ Jesus, Garnet."

Never before had the simple closing of a hand carried so much meaning. Relief poured through him. When the time came to greet his bride, Sam barely grazed her lips with his.

"Father?" Hester tugged on his breeches. "Is she my mama now?"

Garnet stooped down and nodded as she opened her arms.

Hester threw her arms around Garnet's neck. "Chris! Ethan! I have a mama!"

Christopher chuckled. "So do we, you silly goose. She's our mother now, too."

Garnet kept hold of Hester as she straightened up. Hester's little legs wound around Garnet's still-evident waist. Ethan wrapped his arms around Garnet's hips.

"Now there's a fine sight." The parson smiled.

Sam pulled Hester from Garnet and set her down. "You must be careful. You're a big girl, and the wid—" He caught himself. "Your mama's deserving of special consideration."

"I made hasty pudding this morn." Ruth turned slightly to keep the wind from catching her apron and sending it into a wild flutter. "Hester and Mary can come help me dish it up."

"Come, Mama!" Hester tugged Garnet's hand. "Isn't this merry? We're celebrating!"

Thomas Brooks slapped Sam on the back. "You've a good-wife now. Little Hester's delight bodes well. Though the timing is poor, I'm to call you to the council meeting this eve. I've already asked Falcon to be present, as well."

"But it's his wedding night." Christopher flushed brightly after his outburst.

"I'll attend," Sam said as if his son hadn't mentioned that awkward fact.

As soon as they partook of the hasty pudding, Sam loaded his family into the wagon and headed home. After he lifted Garnet down, he traced a finger down her cheek. "You're pale."

She hitched a shoulder, then slid from his reach. Taking

that hint, Sam turned to his sons. "Chris, unhitch the wagon. Ethan, you're to return to work on the deer hide. Hester—"

His daughter stood in the wagon by the edge. Crooking one arm around his neck, she rested her forehead against his. "Father, I get to stay with you forever and always, don't I?"

"Yes, poppet."

She whispered, "Aunt Dorcas told me I'd have to go back. I don't want to. Mama lets me lick the spoons and has me do fun things. We walk out and gather herbs together, and she let me help her oil the eggs and store them so we'll have plenty come winter."

Sam rubbed noses with his daughter.

Hester giggled, then whispered in his ear, "I'm going to card lots and lots and lots of wool. Aunt Dorcas always wanted wool, so I think that'll please Mama—don't you?"

"I'm sure she'll be happy with any help you render." Sam set her down and nudged her toward the house. Glancing at the length of shadows, he had about two hours ere they supped; then he'd go to the council meeting.

Adding another log to the carefully banked fire in the smokehouse, Samuel looked about. Scores of sausages hung from crossbeams. His mouth watered at the thought of enjoying those in the coming months.

Lord, Your bounty fills the root cellar, this smokehouse, and the pegs in the house. I thank You for Your generosity. I thank You, too, for good friends who surround me and keep me from the snares of the wicked. You've returned my daughter to me. That, most of all, matters to me. As for my wife—I confess, Father, that I've married in haste. I failed to seek Your will. I'm tardy in coming to You, but I ask Your blessing on our union. Amen.

Chores kept him busy until Hester called, "Supper's ready!"

Ethan met him just inside the door. "We're having bubble and squeak for supper!"

Looking at Garnet as she finished frying the meal, Sam said, "I'm partial to that."

Ethan grinned. "It really does bubble and squeak, Father. When you tried to make it, it didn't do that. Mama's carrots and cabbage didn't grow limp, and the pork is in fine, thin ribbons instead of funny chunks."

"We are blessed that God has sent her into our lives and home."

The children chattered through dinner, and Sam didn't silence them. Garnet deserved to hear how they welcomed her into their hearts. Then, too, it covered the strain between the two of them. As soon as he finished, Christopher announced, "I'll go saddle Butterfly for you."

"No need." Sam pushed away from the table. "I'll walk."

By the time he arrived at the meeting, both Thomas and Falcon had joined him. The parson opened the meeting with a prayer; then Erasmus Ryder announced, "In the interest of time, I think it best that we address the most pressing issues first. In keeping with Christian charity and familial obligation, my goodwife and I will take back her niece, Hester. Not only that, but Ethan and Christopher should come, as well."

"My children are going nowhere."

Erasmus pointed his finger. "You, Samuel Walsh, cannot deny the woman beneath your roof is with child."

"She's a widow," Thaddeus Laswell said. "Her husband could have sired the babe."

"Not with her belly still so flat," Erasmus shot back.

Alan Cooper rose. "Even though she be with child, I would

take the woman to wife. The reverend has preached on how Hosea married Gomer, knowing full well she was a harlot."

"I doubt any other man would be so accepting." Erasmus spoke so quickly that Sam knew they'd scripted out this little performance. "I'd have us resolve one last matter whilst Walsh is before the council. He's cheated me of wool and coin for my tobacco. I went to him in private, but he refused to part with what he owes me, so I now seek recompense."

"Walsh," Fred Stamsfield said, "how do you answer this charge?"

"I'm grateful for the opportunity to set matters straight, Goodman Stamsfield." Sam looked about the room, making it a point to look each council member in the eyes. "I appreciate Goodman Laswell for crediting the right man for siring the babe. I can state with a clear conscience that I've known but one woman thus far in my life, and 'twas within the sacred bond of marriage."

Sam paused to allow that declaration a moment to sink in, then continued. "As for the widow's condition—indeed, she does not outwardly appear to be with child, but for understandable reason. She was dreadfully ill when I bought her, so she'd lost much flesh. Come spring, when she delivers, those who have misjudged her morals and mine will realize how they've wronged us."

Laswell combed his fingers through his beard. "My goodwife made mention after the first Sunday the widow attended church that she looked exceedingly frail."

"Ample proof that I should wed her." Cooper puffed out his chest like a bantam rooster preparing to spar. "The widow needs to rest, and she cannot do so in a home where three children require attention."

"I'll be sure to mention your kind concerns to her, Goodman Cooper." Samuel couldn't suppress a smile. "I fear it's misplaced, though. This very noon, Garnet Wheelock became my wife."

"That's not possible!" Cooper shot to his feet. "Banns weren't posted or read."

"We all know Samuel has been free to marry. He's been a widower for years now. Since he bought the bride, any reasonable person would understand marriage might well ensue. As for the woman. . ." Reverend Clark shrugged. "Widows are shipped here with the clear understanding that they marry. Samuel possesses legal paperwork, which declares her free of any encumbrances. She's accompanied the Walsh family to services for the past four weeks. I deemed that sufficient declaration of intent on her part, as well."

"I witnessed the marriage," Falcon said.

"As did I," Thomas said. "Though I, myself, would have considered taking such a fine widow as my own wife, I respected Walsh's claim."

"Reverend Clark would not have gone against his good conscience and officiated improperly," Stamsfield said.

"But by law, a widow must be delivered of her child ere she marries again," Alan Cooper snapped. "Isn't that right, Dickson?"

"You were willing to overlook that matter and wed her," Laswell mumbled.

The son of a judge, Dickson had more knowledge of the law than most. His brows beetled as he pondered the situation. "Such laws are in place with specific intent. A man's rightful heirs ought to be his own flesh. Since Samuel has two sons, the addition of a babe would not pose a challenge to their status. In this instance, the pregnancy posed no impediment to marriage."

Falcon snorted. "This whole meeting is an affront."

As head of the council, Dickson turned to Erasmus Ryder. "You cannot fault a man for keeping a woman to whom he's not married beneath his roof, then fault him for wedding her in the next."

"They weren't wed when I called a meeting," Ryder pointed out. "My concern was for my niece and nephews."

Sam seriously doubted the veracity of his brother-in-law's assertion, but he chose not to dwell on it at the moment. Clearly, his children would remain in his keeping. "With those matters settled, I challenge Erasmus Ryder to state his claim against me so I can clear my name."

Erasmus folded his arms akimbo, and his eyes narrowed. "I went to you to collect on debts you owe me, and you refused payment."

"This is a serious charge," Dickson said. "Honorable men discharge their debts. What do you say Walsh owes you?"

Erasmus rested his hands on the table and leaned forward as he enunciated each word with hatred. "Fleeces and cornmeal."

Dickson turned back to Samuel. "Goodman Walsh? How do you respond to this?"

"In the past, I've bartered cornmeal for Ryder's tobacco in order to meet my tithe and tax obligations." Sam hitched his shoulder. "I made no commitment to him to do so this year, and as he's known for growing good-quality Virginia tobacco, he's able to sell it elsewhere."

Dickson drummed his fingers on the tabletop. "How, then, did you meet your tithe and tax obligations?"

"I dealt with Thomas Brooks."

"That makes no sense," Dickson mused aloud. "Surely you would have garnered a more favorable exchange with Ryder since he is family to you."

"Not so." Sam looked at Erasmus and revealed, "Ryder always demanded and received fair market value from me."

"A crop costs me the same to grow no matter who buys it," Erasmus said. "And Walsh just told you all my tobacco is of the finest quality."

"Have you since sold the tobacco you assumed Walsh would buy from you?"

The question barely left Dickson's mouth ere Erasmus spat, "I'm no fool. Of course I did—but I had to journey to do so, and the trip cost me four shillings."

"You cannot hold me at fault for the assumptions you made," Sam said. "And there's not a man here who doesn't incur costs for the business he conducts. I had to travel a day and a half each way to the gristmill, and the miller takes one-sixth of the milling as his portion."

"What about the fleeces?" Ryder's head took on a defiant tilt.

"Shearing is done in spring," Parson Clark frowned. "How can you still owe Ryder wool now?"

"My flock is longwool. I shear the sheep both spring and autumn. The day Dorcas and Erasmus took my Hester to live with them, they took my spring shearing, as well. Since then, each spring and autumn, they've claimed the fleeces as the cost of keeping her for me."

"Your flock has increased by half again in that time." Thomas Brooks shook his head.

"And," Erasmus countered, "the child has grown, as well."

"You sought payment for minding the welfare of your own

niece?" Reverend Clark's voice reflected disbelief.

"Women are scarce, and their time's valuable," Alex Smith stated in Erasmus's defense. "Had Samuel hired someone to mind Hester, it would have cost a pretty penny."

"But had I done so," Sam stated wryly, "you would have brought me before the council and removed Hester from my home. Tonight is ample proof of that."

Smith sighed. " 'Tis true. No matter which route you chose, someone could find fault."

"My goodwife always passes our Mary's clothing down to Hester. Her shoes, as well." Falcon arched a brow. "Ryder, was it such a burden to feed one small child?"

"None of this is your concern, Morton," Alan Cooper rasped.

"Nor is it yours, Cooper," Samuel said. He then looked at the council. "But I state it clearly here: My sheep average slightly over fourteen pounds of wool apiece each year. Multiply that by eighteen, and 'tis abundantly clear my daughter's needs posed no hardship on the Ryders."

"Eighteen? But that's your entire flock." Falcon gave Samuel a puzzled look. "Dorcas took Naomi's loom and your spring shearing that year, so I assumed all along that she shared the profit of her weaving with you. Has she not?"

"No."

"Why should she? She does all the labor, and she minded the girl." Erasmus pointed at Samuel. "And you've sheared your sheep again but not given over the fleeces."

"If," Dickson said slowly, "the fleeces were first taken the day Hester went to abide in your home, then he's paid—and dearly, I might add—in advance."

"But who among us would ask payment for watching kin?"

Disgust painted Thomas's face. "At the outset, Ryder said Christian charity and concern motivated him to seek the care of Walsh's children. I'm thinking greed, not charity, is behind all of this."

"My goodwife spins yarn aplenty and knits our wear." One of the newer settlers plucked at his doublet as if to illustrate his point. "We were told looms are forbidden in the New World. Mother England is to receive all raw materials and send them back as bolt goods."

"At a cost none can afford," Brooks muttered.

Dickson let out a sigh. "Reverend Clark, almost a score of years ago, we met o'er this very issue. By sending all our wool, flax, and cotton to England, we doomed our citizens. The cost of the cloth they sent back was so dear that none could afford to clothe their family and blanket their beds.

"Throughout England, families own looms and weave homespun. As we are all English citizens, that same right ought to belong to us, as well. Surely the law was intended to ward off the start of industrial development here when other endeavors are more important. The council voted if someone wove for family or for charitable means that then the spirit and heart of the law were met."

"Thank you for that explanation, Goodman Dickson." The parson nodded. "Christ admonished us to render unto Caesar what is Caesar's and unto God what is God's. By paying taxes and tithes, you fulfill His instruction. I am not a scholar of the law. What I would say is that each man is responsible before the Lord for his family's needs and conduct."

"It occurs to me," Smith said, "that Goodwife Ryder has gone beyond simply providing for her family's private need and uses the loom as a business enterprise."

Dickson turned to Smith. "A point well made. One we need to address."

"The solution is plain enough." Falcon gestured toward Samuel. "Sam was generous to allow Dorcas the use of the loom these many years. Now that he's wed, the loom rightfully belongs back in his household. I'm sure his bride has need of it."

Erasmus let out a roar. "Now see here!"

"I, for one, agree." Stamsfield looked about the table. "What say the rest of the council?"

Erasmus fumed, "You overstep your authority in seeking to interfere with family affairs."

"Citing familial concern, you brought me before the council, Goodman Ryder." Sam folded his arms across his chest. "Once the matter came to this assemblage, you implicitly agreed to abide by the council's decision—just as you expected I would have to."

"This would rob me of coin!"

Sam stared at him. "You worry about money. I came to fight for my family."

fourteen

Garnet sat at the spinning wheel and kept her hands busy. Unsettled by the day's events, she tried to reassure herself that she'd done the right thing by marrying Samuel. Compared to Alan Cooper, her groom was a prince. From the day Samuel had purchased her, he'd treated her with respect.

But he doesn't want my child.

She lost the rhythm of pressing the pedal and pulling on the fibers.

"Mama?" Hester set aside the carding brushes. "Will you walk me to the privy? It's so dark."

Christopher whispered something in Ethan's ear as Garnet led Hester outside.

When she and Hester returned, Sam stood in the open doorway. He looked years younger as he smiled. "God went before me. All is well."

Garnet slipped past him and busied herself at the spinning wheel once again. Hearing all went well for him pleased her. Sweet Hester had used every opportunity to call her "Mama" all afternoon, and relief filled Garnet in knowing the council hadn't broken the little girl's heart.

"Mama and me—we've been keeping each other company, Father. I'm carding the wool, and she's spinning it. Look how much we got done!"

Samuel leaned against the edge of the stones that formed the fireplace. "Hester, you've nigh unto filled that basket with carded wool, and it's rolled in such a way that it stays straight. Mind you, I'm not much of a judge of these things, but it all looks excellent to me. And look at your mama's bobbin. She spins with a deft hand, don't you agree?"

Hester beamed her agreement.

Ethan shifted from one foot to the other. "Father?"

Samuel ruffled Ethan's hair. "Yes?"

"The wid—I mean, Mother made Christopher a new shirt and a bodice for Hester. We're curing that deer hide so she can stitch you buckskin breeches. Will the cloth she weaves be for a shirt for me?"

Samuel's smile faded. "I cannot say. Her babe will require blankets and swaddling clothes. Those needs most likely will come ahead of your desires."

"Oh." Ethan's mouth drooped.

Resting a hand on his son's thin shoulder, Samuel said, "Take a lesson from this. As a man, you must sometimes put aside your own desires for the sake of another's needs. Not a one of us gets everything he wants in life. You must learn to be satisfied with your lot."

Every last word her new husband uttered drove a stake of pain through Garnet's soul. He'd not tried to be diplomatic in the least. Samuel Walsh was keeping his promise to make sure her child would be provided for—but at what cost? It wouldn't take many such comments to turn his children's hearts against the babe.

Christopher stretched and pretended to yawn. "It's bedtime."

Ethan brightened. "We have a surprise for you!"

"I want to tell it!" The carding brushes clattered from Hester's hands onto the floor. "I'm not a baby anymore."

"So she's moving upstairs with us," Ethan chimed in.

The spinning wheel stopped, and the yarn broke as Garnet heard their announcement.

"Ethan and I snuck the mattress off the trundle and toted it up the ladder whilst Mama took Hester out to the privy." Christopher stood straight as a lance. "I'll listen to their scripture verses tonight so you don't have to trouble yourselves with us."

"Actually, Chris, I'm going to need your help." Samuel's voice started out at a croak and quickly normalized. "Goodman Laswell is to arrive soon."

"Why would he come at night?"

Garnet wondered the same thing.

Samuel folded his arms across his chest. "He and some other men are bringing over the loom."

"You bought a loom today?" Ethan gaped at his father.

"No, no. Long ago, I bought it for your mother. Your aunt Dorcas borrowed it. Now that we have a woman, we'll have need of it again." He looked at Garnet. "Since it's so large, I thought to put it in the barn until you've spun enough to weave. Does that meet with your approval?"

Garnet nodded her head while promising herself she'd work diligently so she'd soon have use of the loom and make sufficient for a shirt for Ethan, as well as clothing for her baby. With that on her mind, she joined the ends of the thread together and started the wheel in motion.

Her thoughts spun as fast as the wheel, leaving her slightly dizzy. *I need to spin each morn and eve, and at any other moment I can spare. I've yet much to preserve. Ruth offered us some of their pears. Drying pears will take a few days' work, but 'twill be well worth the effort in the dead of winter. I could trade her cheese for them.*

Cheese—by the beginning of next month, the cow will go dry. Since Samuel slaughtered the hog, I've not had to pour the excess milk into the swill and have been able to make more wheels. Cheese keeps well, and from what Samuel said, most around here don't make cheese. Instead of buying it from the northern colonies, they could purchase it from us.

A big, strong hand halted the spinning wheel. "Garnet? You were lost deep in thought. The wagon bearing the loom has arrived. They took far less time than I expected." The children ran outside, but Sam didn't immediately follow them.

"Garnet, I would have you know that Goodman Dickson insisted upon the loom coming to us this very night. Erasmus Ryder was sorely vexed that his wife would no longer be permitted to weave for profit. To assure that no damage came to the loom, the men of the council went together and have brought it hence."

She'd used the slate to write to the boys earlier in the evening. Garnet lifted it from beside her stool and wrote, *Give cheese to thank?*

"That's a fine notion. Bring a knife with you. We'll cut one of the wheels and give each man a share."

Moonlight assisted the men in the yard; by the time they moved the loom inside the barn, Garnet and Ethan had lit four oil lamps. Christopher dragged a chest, a crate, and a pair of barrels away from a wall to make sufficient space for the loom.

Garnet counted seven men, but she'd already given the parson a small wheel of cheese that afternoon, so she selected a fair-sized wheel and cut it into sixths as the men carefully set the loom out of the way.

"Felicitations on your marriage, Goodwife Walsh," an older man said as he turned around. He reared back. "Bless me, is that cheese?"

Garnet nodded.

"Aye. My goodwife asked me to be sure you men received our thanks for your help this eve." Sam motioned to her.

Following his direction, Garnet approached the eldest first, then gave each man his portion. Reverend Clark grinned. "I've already enjoyed some of your delicious cheese, Goodwife Walsh. The flavor went especially well with an apple."

"You've a goodly supply of cheese there." One of the men gave Samuel an assessing look. "I'd not be averse to bartering for some."

"I'd gladly deal with you, as well," another said.

"Garnet and I will discuss the matter."

The eldest looked perplexed. "How can you discuss anything when she's mute?"

Someone else let out a bark of a laugh. "I have yet to meet a woman who couldn't make everyone know her mind."

"My goodwife is exceedingly expressive with her gestures, and she also writes on a slate." Samuel moved to stand beside her. "But I speak for us both when I thank you all."

The men took their leave, and Garnet headed back toward the house. Christopher tried to steer Hester to the opposite side of the house.

"Mama has to plait my hair so it won't tangle whilst I sleep." Hester slid her hand into Garnet's.

Relieved to stretch out the time before she and Samuel were alone, Garnet nodded. Once in the keeping room, she ran the comb through Hester's dark hair over and over, then divided it into three sections and plaited it.

Sam pulled the stool over to the middle of the room, stood on it, and pushed up on a section of the ceiling boards. Ruth had been right—a door existed there. "Chris," he said, " 'Tis silly for Hester to go outside and climb the ladder when I can lift her from here."

Hester wrapped her arms about Garnet. "This is the best day of my life! I have you for my mama, and I'm grown up enough to be upstairs."

As Sam lifted the little girl up to Chris, Garnet headed back to the spinning wheel. Wood scraped; then the segment thumped into place, leaving her alone with her groom. Garnet fumbled with the carded wool and hastily started spinning.

"The children ought sleep well tonight. They've stayed up far past the time they usually go to bed."

Garnet didn't look up. She merely nodded.

"I planted very little flax this year—something I now regret. As you like to spin and knit, more flax would have allowed you to make linen and linsey-woolsey." He went on to identify some items he felt the farm needed and what he felt could be bartered away. Finally, he decided, "The hour grows late. Cease spinning, and we'll retire."

Pulling back the covers on the bed, he cleared his throat. "It's been four years since Naomi passed on."

Garnet shuddered.

"I tell you this because my nightshirt fell to pieces awhile back. 'Twas beyond redemption, so I—" He halted and gave her a stunned look. "Here I am, confessing I've no nightshirt, yet I'm sure you must have returned Ruth's nightdress to her. What have you been wearing to bed?"

Heat enveloped her. Garnet didn't want to confess she'd been sleeping in a petticoat.

"None of that now. Blushing is for maidens." He towed her toward the door. "Grab the lamp. We'll find something that will suffice."

They ended up in the barn, and Samuel knelt by one of the boxes Christopher had moved to create space for the loom. "I've been remiss in offering these things to you. Here." The leather hinges of the box crackled as he opened it. "It's been so long since I had a female under the roof that I no longer recalled the feminine things a woman desires."

Garnet peered over his shoulder. He pushed a hairbrush off to the side. Next, he took out a pair of stockings that would help keep her warm during the winter months. The stockings Garnet currently wore were carefully darned but so threadbare they wouldn't last much longer.

"Ah. Ruth made this for Naomi." Insubstantial as air and prettier than a handful of snowflakes, the shawl he removed would be for fine occasions and church. Surely it wouldn't keep her warm. Sam studied it a moment, then nodded. " 'Twill serve you well whilst you suckle your babe."

Your babe. Though he'd not emphasized the word, his meaning still came through. Garnet rested her hand over her waist, as if to protect the child she carried.

Oblivious to her concern, he set aside a rabbit-fur muff and a cape of two tones of blue. Tails of fabric from two smallish folded squares were likely aprons. Sam then lifted a yellowed-with-age nightdress from the bottom of the trunk. It unfolded, but as he held the garment over the trunk, the hem stayed clean. "As I recall, the aprons and this belonged to Naomi's mother. She was a smallish woman like you."

Garnet mouthed, *Thank you.*

Sweeping everything back into the box, Sam said, "I'll

carry this chest in for you. Mary Morton used to stand on one of similar size. Falcon built it to raise her up to the table so she could help her mother with cooking. Hester enjoys being at your side. This will enable her to assist you."

Garnet held the lamp as Sam carried the box back to the house. Every step demanded her courage. *We married out of necessity, but he is trying to provide for me. Cecil drank himself under the table at our wedding supper. Compared to that, this is a vast improvement.*

A movement caught Garnet's attention.

"Garnet, open the door latch."

Samuel's words barely made it past the pounding in her ears. A scream welled up.

fifteen

Sam dropped the box and whipped around. Garnet's shrill scream wavered in the crisp night air, but he saw no danger. "Garnet—"

She shuffled back.

Sam grabbed her with one hand and the lamp with his other. Garnet tried to twist away. He blew out the flame and hastily thumped the oil lamp down on the box while still manacling her wrist in an unyielding grip.

Another scream welled up and burst out of her.

Sam squinted in the direction she was staring and saw nothing more than a rat scurrying away. *But 'twas a field mouse that caused her to panic that other time.*

For a small woman, she fought his restraint with astonishing might. Sam clenched her wrist more securely and yanked her against himself. Wrapping his other arm about her shoulders, he dipped his head so his mouth would be next to her ear. "Garnet. Garnet, 'tis gone. It's gone now. All gone. It ran off."

Terror left her stiff, but Sam counted that as a vast improvement. She'd ceased screaming and no longer tried to break free from him.

"You're safe. Hear me, Garnet. 'Tis gone." He turned loose of her wrist and wrapped his other arm about her in an unyielding hold.

She whimpered a single word, shuddered, and swooned.

Sam swept her up, carried her into the keeping room, and laid her on the bed. Flames from the hearth gave a soft glow to the room, yielding light and warmth, so he left her only long enough to pull in the box and lantern, then latch the door.

Help. She'd finally spoken, and the word was a plea wrought with nothing short of terror. *Help*. Admittedly, beady-eyed rats weren't welcome, but why would she hold such fear of a common rodent?

He pulled off her mobcap, then removed her slippers and stockings. Her stockings—they'd been mended in so many spots, 'twas nothing short of astonishing that they stayed together at all. *I'm glad there are stockings in the box I gave to her.*

Sam sat on the edge of the jump bed and chafed her hand. "Garnet? Garnet."

Slowly, her eyelids flickered open. At first, confusion clouded her eyes, but just as quickly, fright filled them.

Her panic tore at him. Clasping her hand firmly between his, Sam said, "You're safe. I promise; you're safe. 'Twas outside, and it's gone." Reassurance flowed from his mouth, and the fright slowly faded from her face, only to be replaced by vulnerability.

He held fast to her hand with one of his, but traced her lips with his other fingers. "You spoke, Garnet. God gave you back your voice."

She said nothing.

Lord, what am I to say to reassure her? Put words in my mouth.

Trailing his fingers through her hair, Sam let out a slow breath. "The day Naomi died, Ruth packed that box. I slammed on the lid and took it out to the barn. I've said the marriage was not a happy one. In truth, 'twas miserable. Keeping Naomi's possessions locked away was my way of putting the bad memories behind me. Now that I've opened the chest and gone clear to the bottom of it, I've found the memories no longer hold sway over me."

Garnet lay perfectly still.

"Something happened. It must have been terrible for you to sacrifice your ability to talk just to tamp down the memory. Just as you stood with me as I opened the lid to the chest, now I'll stay with you. Open your mouth and give voice to the fear. You asked for my help, Garnet. God gave you a gift by returning your voice. Don't turn away from it. Use your voice now, and we will lift the lid on the box of your fear. Once we get to the bottom of it, you'll be free."

Her lips quivered.

Sam continued to hold her hand and stroke her soft hair. "Help. That is what you said to me. You saw something—"

Her whole body went rigid.

Sam cupped her cheek and bent closer. "It was outside. We're inside."

A broken sigh poured out of her.

"On the day you left England, did you still have your voice?"

She nodded.

"Yes. Say yes, Garnet."

"Yes." The single syllable sounded tentative and raspy.

"Well done." He studied her by the fire's light. "The voyage was harsh. The man I bought you from said of the dozen brides, only five survived."

She seemed to shrink right before him. "Chained." Her eyes squeezed shut, yet her hand gripped his with desperation. "Together."

The first word chilled him to the marrow of his bones; the

second left twin streaks of anger and disgust through him.

An ugly sob wracked her. "They died."

Sam pulled her into his arms. The horror he felt in knowing what happened didn't begin to compare with what she'd endured. From her reaction to the rodents, Sam knew what would come next. Holding her securely, he echoed her words. "They died." She shuddered, and he knew how cruel it was to push her—but 'twas also essential. Until she finally purged her mind of the gruesome memory, she'd not break free from the terror that enslaved her. Cradling her head to his shoulder, he said, "They died, and the rats—"

A keening wail tore through her. Words tumbled out between her sobs. "Storm. . .rats! Screamed. . .no help. No help."

Garnet wept and wept. Finally, she slumped against him.

" 'Tis over now, Garnet." He kissed her brow. "Sleep."

She fell headlong into sleep, and Sam tucked her in. He kicked off his boots and removed his doublet but decided to stay in his shirt and breeches. It wasn't much of a wedding night, but it wasn't much of a marriage, either. After a time, he crawled into the bed.

In the still of the room, the fire glowed and occasionally sparked. Night sounds intruded, and there were the occasional odd bumps from the children up in the loft. Then Garnet made a choking sound.

He opened his eyes at once. "Garnet, give me your hand."

Biting her lip, she tried to silence her weeping.

"Garnet, your hand—yield it over to me. If you are fearful of me, please attend and know there is no cause. If you are saddened, then take the comfort a friend offers."

A small, work-chapped hand slid timidly across the mattress.

He engulfed her hand in his. Hers was too thin by half and shook. Samuel noted both facts with a measure of dismay. He whispered in a deep rasp, "Slumber now, Garnet. No harm shall come to you in my care. I vow it."

He held that hand until it went limp from her falling asleep. Still, he let it rest on their corn-husk mattress and covered it with his own big, capable hand. Should she awaken, there would be that sign of his concern for her. He should have gone to sleep straight off, for he was markedly tired, but something had happened that made it impossible. He'd caught himself just a breath away from kissing the backs of her fingers.

❧

A blast of cool air awakened Garnet. She blinked. *Why am I on this side of the bed?* Memories of the previous day welled up. She gasped and turned her head in time to watch Samuel shut the door.

He glanced at the bed and smiled. "So you're awake." Setting the milk pail on the table, he chuckled. "Ethan laid snares yesternoon all by himself. He'll be impossibly proud of himself when he checks them."

Realizing she was dressed beneath the bedclothes, Garnet slid from the mattress and made the bed.

Warm, heavy hands touched her shoulders and turned her. "It would be wise for us to discuss bartering. Our neighbors will all know of your fine cheese and want to trade for it. What say you?"

Garnet nodded.

"Give voice to your thoughts," he urged quietly.

Last night hadn't been a dream? Had she regained her ability to speak? Garnet hesitated, then whispered, "Breakfast?"

Her husband smiled. "I'd ask you to make stirabout. I always burned it, but yours carries a fine flavor. What do you add to it?"

"Molasses or honey." She moistened her lips. "More honey? Rice?"

"The Carolina Colony grows rice aplenty. Laswell has connections to someone from there. Obtaining rice will be easy enough. As for honey—I'll ask Falcon. Last year, he found a stump brimming with honey. Not only did Ruth have honey to trade, but beeswax, as well."

"Ruth." Garnet felt a wave of warmth just from thinking of what a dear friend her neighbor had become. "Want her to have cheese. Generous."

"Are you telling me to be generous in the barter, or are you saying Ruth is generous?"

Garnet caught herself as she started to nod. "Both."

Samuel chuckled.

Since he was in a good mood, Garnet hesitated to ask the next question, but it still needed to be asked. "Owe any debts?"

"Not a one." He rubbed his forehead. "I've grown lazy about knowing what foodstuffs we have on hand. Since you took over cooking, all I've done is enjoy the meals and not paid attention to our supplies. In addition to honey and rice, what have we need of?"

"Oats?"

"Much as I like your stirabout, I should have anticipated that answer. Dickson grows oats. He has two indentured servants who help considerably, but men rarely trouble themselves over domestic chores. Betwixt your cheese and soap, I estimate Dickson will strike a deal quite gladly."

"Crocks of cheese." Her voice sounded funny, but Garnet

continued on. "Sheep's cheese. In the springhouse."

His brows rose. "As much as Hester chatters, I'm surprised she didn't tell me all about that venture."

"Made it while children are at school."

He looked at the pegs in the ceiling and shook his head. "Your industry surpasses imagination." His gaze fell to her belly, and his tone went flat. "I suppose it's a good thing. The last days before having a babe, women slow down. You'll be abed for a solid month after delivering, too."

Garnet turned away and started breakfast.

Samuel rapped his knuckles on a tin pan as he did each morning to wake the children. "Up with you!" he announced.

The door to the second story slid open. "Hester left her shoes down there last night."

"Hurry! I have to go to the privy!"

Garnet located Hester's shoes as Sam reached up. "Hester, cease your wiggling and giggling, and I'll bring you down." As soon as he had her in his arms, Sam turned his daughter and snuggled her as if he'd never held anything more precious. "Don't fret over shoes, Garnet. I'll just carry her this morn."

Once he stepped out the door, Garnet set Hester's shoes on the crate. The soft thump echoed the heaviness in her heart. *He'll cherish his own children, but he'll merely tolerate mine. Lord, I don't know what to do.*

sixteen

As he carried Hester back into the house, Sam tugged on her braid. "Something special happened."

"You got married!"

"Yes, well. . .that's right, I did." He shut the door and bent to set her down.

"And now I got a mama."

He nodded.

"Mama does that, too—nods her head." Hester danced from one foot to the other. "That means you are the same. That's why you got married. Schoolmaster Smith said things that are alike belong together."

"You need to get dressed. It'll be breakfast time soon, and then you'll be off to school."

Once they all gathered around the table, Sam bowed his head and prayed. "Most loving Father, we thank You for the bounty You've bestowed upon us. Thank You, too, for the special gift You brought last night. Be with my children at school today. Let them be attentive and return home safely. Amen."

"What special gift?" Hester asked as she grabbed her spoon.

Christopher choked and turned crimson.

"The loom—remember?" Ethan plopped a dollop of butter on his stirabout.

"Actually, I wasn't referring to the loom, though I'm glad to have it back." Sam motioned to Garnet. "Why don't you tell them about it?"

"I'll get my slate." Ethan popped up.

Garnet reached over and stopped him. "No. Thank you."

"You talked!" Christopher half shouted in surprise.

"Oh no." Ethan slumped down. "Now Aunt Dorcas is going to want the recorder back because the wi—because Mother can sing at church."

"She can't have it, can she, Father?" Christopher rested his elbows on the table. "If we got the loom back, that means the council believes anything that belonged to Mother belongs to. . ." Christopher cast a look at Garnet.

"Mama," Hester supplied. She beamed. "Mary Morton calls her mother 'Mama,' and I always envied her. Was it sinful for me, Father? I wanted my own mama. Now I have one."

"One of the commandments exhorts us not to covet." Sam looked at his bride. "We are to be satisfied with our lot in life. Life rarely brings you what you want."

To his dismay, Garnet slowly nodded.

Over the next three weeks, everyone stayed excessively busy. Just as the creatures hoarded food for the winter, so everyone labored to extract each last morsel of food from the earth. Neighbors arrived in hopes of bartering for Garnet's cheese. Ruth Morton came over thrice a week with the excess from her cow, and Thomas Brooks sent his along, as well. They'd agreed that half of the cheese made from their milk would belong to them; the other half was Garnet's.

"Garnet?" Sam cleared his throat. "Goodman Dickson is here. He'd like some cheese."

Garnet sat at the spinning wheel and continued to work. "Deal with him as you will."

"Is there aught you need?"

"I've flax and fleeces aplenty. I trust you to do what's best."

"Very well." She'd been strangely remote since their marriage. Just yestermorn, he'd seen her placing her palm on her belly, measuring the small mound that finally testified to impending motherhood. She'd not known Sam was there, and the strained look on her face warned him not to make his presence known. Garnet chose not to say much of her former husband other than he'd shown a weakness for both spirits and cards. The day the sheriff arrived to take him to debtors' prison, he'd keeled over dead. She never spoke of the babe. Sam took his cue from her and didn't, either.

Sam left her in the keeping room and went back to the barn.

"So what does your goodwife name as the price of her cheese?"

"She left that to me. What do you offer?"

They settled on the payment of a small, tin-punched lantern. As Dickson prepared to leave, he squinted at Sam. "Has it occurred to you that your goodwife hides away in your keeping room? The only time I see her is at worship."

"She's spinning much of the time. In truth, it puts me in mind of a bird lining the nest ere the young come."

The old man chortled softly as he swung up into his saddle. "Just so. Goodwife Morton isn't finding a need to prepare for her babe—but she's very early on yet, and she's already been through this seven other times."

Sam handed him a wheel of cheese. "Aye, 'tis the truth. Garnet's on her first."

As Dickson left, Sam cast a look back at the cabin. *This babe will be her first, and if things continue on as they have, 'twill be her only. I've no one to blame but myself. Whilst we exchanged vows, I told her 'twas sufficient that we care for each other in Christ Jesus.*

I've always been a man of my word.

Sam bleakly walked toward the nearest field. All about him, the land struggled against the coming winter. Soon life would go dormant, only to burst forth in spring. Garnet would give birth in spring, too. But the only yield she'd ever have would be another man's child.

❧

"Mama, I can't put my arms all the way 'round you anymore." Hester stood on tiptoe and tried once more just to prove her point. "See?"

"Enough of that." Sam shed his cloak and hung it on a peg by the door.

His curt tone of voice made it clear he wanted no reminder of her condition. Garnet tried to hide her sadness. It wasn't right for the children to be caught in the middle of the strain. She straightened the clout covering Hester's hair. "There. Now get back to practicing your letters."

"I'll write my whole alphabet for you." Hester skipped over to the table and picked up her slate. "Ethan, why do you look so sour?"

Garnet braced herself for his answer. Thus far, the children had remained oblivious to the tension between her and Samuel. Try as she might to keep the problem a secret, Garnet knew the time would come when she couldn't shield them from the fact that their father didn't want her child.

"You do look sour," Sam said to his son.

Using his slate pencil to scratch the back of his hand, Ethan let out a gusty sigh. "I'm supposed to figure out how much of a hogshead eight firkins is."

"You can do that." Sam headed toward the table. "It's a fractional problem. There are nine gallons in a firkin. How many gallons in a hogshead?"

As they worked on the arithmetic, Garnet sat by the fire and carefully stitched together the buckskin breeches she'd been making for her husband. Though supple, the leather was difficult to pierce with the needle. Samuel desperately needed these new breeches, though. She hoped to finish them tonight.

Christopher burst through the door and ran toward the hearth. "A huge buck is out where the vegetable garden was!" He reached for the flintlock. "Hurry, Father!"

"No, son." Samuel looked across the keeping room. "Our smokehouse is full. It would be a waste to slaughter the beast when we're not in need of meat. Never take something you cannot use."

Is that how he thinks of me? He bought me because he'd get Hester back from the Ryders. He married me to keep her and the boys. He took me because I suited his needs.

She pushed aside the buckskin and stood. The room tilted crazily.

"Garnet?"

Blinking, she turned and wondered how Samuel got from the other side of the table to her. He curled his hands around her upper arms as she said, "I'm going to add a log to the fire."

"Christopher, see to that." Sam exerted pressure on her arms. "Sit back down. You cannot rise of a sudden like that."

Melting back onto the stool, Garnet tore her gaze from her husband to Christopher. The boy moved the logs about in the fire with an andiron, then added another log. "Thank you, Chris."

"Is she faring better, Father?"

"I'd say so. Her color's come back." Sam studied her, and Garnet couldn't look away. " 'Twas just a passing affliction.

Sometimes when a woman moves too swiftly, this happens." One at a time, his fingers released her arms until his hands hovered close but didn't touch her. "Have a care in rising."

Garnet nodded slowly. As her husband walked back toward the table, she lifted the buckskins back into her lap. *Mayhap I'm being unfair to him. He's shown me nothing but kindness.* It took forceful pushing with the thimble to force the needle through the leather. Garnet shoved it through yet again. *Truly, Samuel treats me well. But what about my child?*

He'd refrained from saying a word about the baby. In the midst of this episode, he'd never once referred to her condition.

"Christopher, have you completed your lessons?" Sam looked up from Ethan's work.

"Aye, I have. I'm to recite Reverend Michael Wigglesworth's 'The Day of Doom' on the morrow."

" 'Tis a long poem. Are you confident?"

Chris stretched to his full height and launched into the fiery passage, putting notable feeling into the piece. When he finished, Hester shivered. "That was scary!"

"Well done," Garnet praised.

"Indeed." Sam's voice held full approval.

"My stomach is growling." Ethan wiggled on the bench.

"You ate two bowls of stew at supper." Christopher folded his arms across his chest. "Just because you snared the hares doesn't mean you have to eat all of them by yourself."

Hester giggled. "Soon Ethan's belly will be as big as Mama's!"

"My hares were plump, but they'd never get me to that size. I'd have to eat a—"

"Silence yourselves." Sam scowled. "If you cannot speak respectfully, hold your tongue."

Ethan's teasing grin twisted into a stricken expression. He'd been told to be silent, so he couldn't say a word. His eyes begged Garnet's forgiveness. Confusion painted Hester's face.

Garnet smiled at them. They'd not meant any disrespect. Still, it would be wrong to disagree with Samuel in front of them. She bowed her head and set to stitching again.

Sam dragged a stool over, stood on it, and opened the ceiling hatch to the upper story. He hopped down, dusted off his hands, and pushed the stool against the far wall. "Chris, come with me. We need to bring in more wood. The weather's turning."

Ethan pushed away from the table. "I'm finished solving the problems. Shall I come along?"

"Put on your cloak." Sam reached for his own as he gave the order.

"I. . ." Ethan puffed his cheeks full of air and let it out in a slow, loud blow. "I left my cloak at school."

"You're ten, Ethan. Fast becoming a man." Sam shook his head. "You cannot indulge in such irresponsibility. The night's too cold for you to be out for more than a few minutes. Your brother and I will have to leave you behind and do this chore without you."

"I'm ready," Christopher said as he fastened the horn button at the throat of his own cloak.

Sam and Christopher went outside. Garnet finished the last stitch in the breeches, knotted her thread, and bit off the excess. She set her work aside and put towels on a stool close by the fire.

"Mama, why did you do that?"

"Rain is on the way. Your brothers might get wet when they climb up the ladder to go to bed. The towels will dry and warm them."

Ethan stared at the fire. "So you think it's going to rain, too?"

"Aunt Dorcas always said she could tell when it would rain. She could feel it in her bones." Hester's face puckered, and she used the tip of her finger to erase something on her slate.

"I don't feel it in my bones," Garnet said as she scooted the towels a little closer to the fire, "but I trust your father. He's very knowledgeable about the land and weather."

Hester let out a moan. "I can't fit the whole alphabet on here."

Garnet studied the carefully written letters. "You've scribed quite a few and nicely. I'd rather see you do your best work than to hurry through. You don't want to get into a habit of being messy."

Ethan wrinkled his nose. "Schoolmaster Smith read from *Poor Richard's Almanack* today. Benjamin Franklin said, ' 'Tis easier to prevent bad habits than to break them.' "

"Exactly. Very nicely said, Ethan. Hester, it's time to be thinking of putting you to bed."

"Will you please take me to the privy?"

"Of course, I will." Garnet slipped into the double-toned blue cape. Though Hester was afraid of the dark and didn't go out alone, something in her voice let Garnet know her little daughter wanted to say something. "Here." She buttoned Hester's cape and tickled her little nose.

Contrary to her usual giggle, Hester remained somber. She waited until she'd finished in the privy, then stood in a weak moonbeam and gave Garnet a woebegone look. "Goodman Morton tells his goodwife that she is fat and sassy. Mary laughs and says it is good when a woman's belly grows big."

"It's a sign that all is well." Garnet chose her words carefully. "Sometimes we pray together and give the Lord our thanks. Other times we whisper our prayers when we're alone. So it is when a woman is with child. Some feel free to celebrate with everyone. Others think it more fitting to be private."

"Oh." Hester slid her hand into Garnet's. "But it was just us, in our own home. No one else heard us say anything about how big your belly is."

"Even so, you must honor your father." As soon as the words exited her lips, Garnet felt a bolt of conviction. *It's my place to honor my husband. I've been sulking instead of thanking the Lord for His provision.*

"Yes, Mama. I will."

They returned to the house, but the keeping room was empty. A few minutes later, Sam and Christopher pulled a sledge to the cabin and started carrying in armloads of wood. "I meant to stack wood on the side of the house, but the weather's gotten ahead of me."

"But you brought gracious plenty," Garnet said. "Thank you." A minute later, she walked to the door and peered out. "Samuel, where's Ethan?"

"Isn't he in the house?"

"Not unless he went to bed."

Sam carried in another load of logs. "Chris, climb up and check on your brother."

A minute later, Christopher stuck his head down through the hatch. "Ethan's not up here."

seventeen

"Sam!" Garnet grabbed his hand and yanked as if her horrified tone hadn't already garnered his attention. "The water buckets are gone!"

"Ethan!" Sam broke away from Garnet and ran toward the stream. "Ethan!"

Christopher sprinted alongside him, shouting for his brother.

One bucket sat on the shore. Moonlight tipped small ripples in the water, but Sam couldn't see Ethan. "Lord—my son!" Sam cried out in anguish as he jogged along the water's edge, searching.

"Father!" Christopher pointed.

Sam dove into the water. Half a dozen powerful strokes took him to his son. Ethan's head bobbed above the water, but Sam clutched him and headed for shore.

Ethan spluttered and coughed—the sweetest sounds Sam had ever heard. "I have you. I have you." Sam lifted Ethan into Chris's waiting arms, then pulled himself out of the cold water and onto land.

"Ethan!" Panic lent an edge to Garnet's voice.

"We found him," Christopher shouted.

"Wet, but well," Sam added as he grabbed Ethan from Chris's arms.

"Lord be praised!" Garnet huffed breathlessly as she reached them. "Here." She swept off her cape and stood on tiptoe to try to envelop him and Ethan in its folds.

Sam stepped back. "Put that back on out here. It'll only get wet, and the last thing we need is for you to sicken again."

It seemed as if it had taken forever for him to run to the stream and reach Ethan. It took no more than a blink but that they were inside the keeping room once again.

"Mama, I did what you told me to." Hester peeked down at them from the hatch door. "Here."

"Good girl!" Garnet caught Ethan's nightshirt as Sam grabbed Hester and lowered her to the floor. "Ethan, get out of those wet things and put this on. Samuel, I finished your buckskins. You change, too."

Sam ignored her order and yanked off Ethan's sodden shirt. Garnet immediately enveloped Ethan in one of the towels.

"Sam, there's another towel to the left of the fire."

He grabbed the towel and started to rumple it through his son's hair. Garnet made an impatient sound. "Samuel, dry off. I'll take care of him."

"He's my son!"

Garnet jerked backward into the spinning wheel, but Christopher grabbed her ere she fell. The spinning wheel toppled over. The clattering sound it made as it tangled with the andirons didn't cover an ominous crack.

"Oh, dear." Hester's little voice whispered in the utterly silent keeping room.

"Are you all right?" Sam stared at his wife.

She nodded and turned away.

Christopher righted the spinning wheel. One of the spokes stuck out at an odd angle, the beautifully turned wood now cracked. "Goodwife Stamsfield's wheel is missing a spoke," Christopher said in an appeasing tone. "She claims it still works fine."

"Father, you're going to wear my hair off my head!"

Sam forced a chuckle and stopped rubbing Ethan's hair. "Change into your nightshirt."

Christopher shot a look from Garnet to him and back again. Worry dug furrows on either side of his mouth. "I'll bring in some more logs while you dry off, Father."

Reaching up, Garnet took a small bundle of herbs from a peg. By the time Sam dried off and had donned his new buckskins, she was setting cups on the table. "Hester, please fetch the honey."

Hester did so, then stood upon the box and asked, "What did you brew?"

"Bee balm tea. Do you like how it smells?"

"It smells pretty. Aunt Dorcas made lots of chicory tea." Her little nose wrinkled. "I didn't like it."

Christopher came back inside, his arms full. "These are the last logs from the sledge, and not a moment too soon. It's starting to rain."

"Some tea will warm you up." Garnet drizzled honey into the teapot, stirred it, and filled cups. "Here you are."

Sam frowned. "Garnet, there are only four cups."

The saddest smile he'd ever seen sketched across her face. "Ruth mentioned I oughtn't drink bee balm."

How she managed it, Sam wasn't quite sure. The mattress from the trundle barely fit through the hatch, but Garnet and Hester now huddled on it beneath a blanket whilst Ethan and Christopher climbed into the jump bed. Sam wanted to draw his wife aside for a private conversation, but with the children underfoot, he'd not yet managed to do so. Now it was too late.

"Garnet, are you warm enough?"

She nodded. "Be sure to keep Ethan bundled up. I don't

want either of you to take a chill."

Giggles spilled out of Hester. "Mama! How did you do that?"

Ethan propped up on one elbow. "What did she do?"

"She has her arms 'round me, but her tummy bumped on my back like someone knocking on the door."

"It's her baby." Christopher gave the explanation in a matter-of-fact tone.

"It's not fair." Hester sat up. "How come Mama's baby isn't my baby, too? Mary said her mama and father share their baby with everyone in the family."

"That's different. Aunt Dorcas—"

"Hush, Ethan," Christopher hissed. "She was wrong about the recorder and about the loom. I—"

"Have you spoken to your aunt recently?" Sam fought to keep his tone even.

"She brought us cookies. After school," Hester said.

"And she said she'd bake us cookies when we decided to come live with her," Ethan added.

"Why," Sam gritted, "would you go live with her?"

"Because," Hester said, "she said Mama's not really our mama and when she has her baby, she won't care about us anymore."

"Well, she's wrong." Garnet's voice rang with certainty.

Hester continued. "I know. Aunt Dorcas was wrong about other things, too. She said I'll always be her baby, but I told her I'm a big girl now. I go to school and sleep upstairs."

"The only place you're going is to sleep." Sam strove to contain his temper. "Hester, lie back down."

Hester flopped down and squirmed beneath the covers. A second later, she whispered loudly, "Mama? Will you make a girl baby? I want a sister."

"The Almighty will decide what to give us." From the way the blanket moved, Sam knew she'd pulled Hester closer and kept an arm around her. "Know this, Hester. You are very dear to me. When the baby comes, God will add love in my heart so there's plenty for everyone."

"Add?" Glee bubbled out of his daughter. "Like when Schoolmaster Smith does the plus instead of the take-away sign!"

"So put your mind to rest." Garnet's head came off the pillow so she could look up at the jump bed. "Our Lord let us keep Ethan so we can all be together. No one can pull us asunder."

"Like when you married Father," Ethan said sleepily. "What God hath joined together, let no man pull asunder."

"But Aunt Dorcas is a woman."

"She's married, Hester," Christopher reasoned. "In God's eyes, a man and a woman are one. They become a team—like two horses pulling a wagon instead of just one."

"When I married your father, I knew he had three fine children in his wagon." Garnet spoke very softly. "When we wed, you became mine."

"I'm glad." Hester snuggled into the pillow.

"Me, too," Sam said. He waited for Garnet to react, but she didn't.

eighteen

The door opened, and Garnet looked up. Christopher stepped inside and shut the door behind himself. "The cow's gone dry."

She forced a smile. "I've been expecting that to happen."

He held up a basket. "I gathered the eggs."

"Thank you. Breakfast is ready." Garnet didn't ask about his father. Sam hadn't gone to bed at all last night. He'd sat before the fireplace, brooding for the longest while; then he took his cloak and went outside. He'd not come back. She didn't know where he was.

"Since we're having stirabout," Ethan asked between bites, "what are you going to do with the eggs?"

"Do you think, perchance, you could fetch me a pumpkin from the barn ere you leave for school?"

"I'm done eating. I'll get it now!" Ethan raced out the door. A few minutes later, he returned with a good-sized pumpkin. "Father is busy. He doesn't want you out in the barn."

Garnet pretended that news didn't wound her. Instead, she thanked Ethan for the pumpkin. A few minutes later, she stood in the doorway and waved as the children set off for school. Once they were out of sight, she shut the door and drew in a deep breath to steady herself.

It took no time at all to clean up from breakfast, and she set to making the pumpkin custard Samuel liked so much. It would take the last of the cream she'd stored in the springhouse. She slipped the two-toned blue cape around her shoulders and fetched the cream.

On the way back to the house, Garnet made a point of not looking at the barn. *Lord, I've been too busy looking upon my husband instead of keeping my eyes on You. I let discontentment come into my heart when I should have been praising You for all You've given me. Starting right now, I'm going to rely upon Your promise in the Bible that if I seek You first, all of the other things will be added unto me.*

She went back into the keeping room. As she poured the custard into the pumpkin shell, Garnet inhaled deeply. The fragrance of the mixture was pleasing.

I'm like the eggs. I was broken and was beaten, but God added sweetness to my life and set me in a new place. The heat—it's like a refiner's fire. I have to trust Him that all will turn out well in the end.

As she stirred up the fire, the door opened. "Mama?"

"Chris!"

"I've sent Ethan and Hester on with the Morton children. I came back because a few things need to be said. First, I'm glad you're our mother now. Father speaks well of others and won't speak ill of anyone. He speaks not at all of my mother. My memories of her are of her being quarrelsome, so I've followed Father's example and not said anything, either."

"I'm sorry, Christopher."

"That was in the past, and nothing can alter it." He puffed out his chest. "I'm not going to school this morning because I'm going to go to Uncle Erasmus, man-to-man."

"No," Samuel pushed the door wide open, "you're not."

❧

Sam clapped a hand onto Chris's shoulder. "I'll put things in order. You belong at school."

Christopher looked at Garnet. "I meant what I said—I'm glad you're our mother." He left and shut the door.

As soon as the latch slid closed, Garnet turned back to the fire and lifted a cauldron.

"That's too heavy for you." Sam strode over and took it from her. He spied the pumpkin inside and gave her a long look.

"I used the cream I had left in the springhouse. It'll be the last pumpkin custard."

Sam lifted the cauldron onto the hook over the fire. "We'll all enjoy it, just as we appreciate all you do." He took Garnet's elbow and led her over to the table. "Sit. I need to speak with you."

She sank down onto a bench, but Sam felt too restless to join her. Instead, he paced toward the jump bed, turned, and approached her once again. "I spent the night in deep thought and prayer. I must speak some harsh truths."

Her face grew grim.

"I wed you because Erasmus forced me to in order to keep my children—or so I thought. But I gave him credit when 'twas not his. God brought you here before Erasmus Ryder thought up his schemes. The Lord merely allowed those schemes to unfold because He can redeem good from wickedness.

"I've spent years now rearing my sons. Protecting them—I do it naturally. Last night, you said when you'd wed me that my children became yours. 'Twas a bittersweet truth I pondered o'er most of the night. Sweet, because memory after memory came to mind of how you've shown your love for them—the praise you gave Christopher for driving the wagon so smoothly, the glee on Ethan's face when you call him over to lick a spoon, and the way you hold Hester's hand in yours as you walk."

"I love your children."

"I know. The bitter part of this is hard for me to confess."

Garnet sat a little straighter. Her hands—the way they moved to try to cover her belly—wrenched his heart. Sam straddled the bench and put his hands atop hers, and she gave him a startled look.

"I'd be lying to say I was happy to learn you were with child. It came as a shock to you, too. You've not said a word about this babe, and I tried to respect your silence by giving you time to accustom yourself to its arrival. Last night is the first time you've acknowledged you're carrying a life. You said God would add love. When the times comes, I have faith that He will fill you with love for this little one."

"He already has." Beneath his palms, he felt how she gently stroked her thumbs back and forth over the child she carried. "I'm blessed to have him."

Sam sat for a while and let that sweet truth fill the silence. Finally, he took a deep breath and looked at her earnestly. "In truth, I've worried I could not love this babe. 'Tisn't flesh of my flesh." The wounded look in her eyes tore at him. He hastened on. "But then I realized Naomi never gave her heart to our children; you have. 'Twasn't the blood tie that mattered. Then, too, there was Joseph. Joseph didn't sire Jesus, yet the Lord put His Son into Joseph's caring. God put your babe into my care."

"You promised to provide—"

"And a beggar's promise that was. It ate at me all night long." He reached between his shirt and doublet and pulled out what he'd worked on. "This is from the spinning wheel.

The wood split badly, but I glued it back together. 'Tis smooth and probably stronger now than the other spokes."

Garnet looked confused.

Sam turned the piece so she could see what he'd done. "Look here. I carved a heart on it. I've not used words that will be lost in time. I carved this here, and it is past time I spoke to you of my love. Since you came, I've been so relieved that Hester is home and life has gone well, I didn't stop to recognize the truth. You filled my home with happiness. Not only that, Garnet—somehow, you filled my heart with love."

Sam placed the spoke in her hands and curled his fingers around hers. "We were both broken souls when God glued us together. Together, we are whole. God willing, we will have as many children together as there are spokes on your spinning wheel—but this is to remind you always that my heart is yours, and I will cherish this first child you carry."

Tears filled her eyes, making them glisten like just-polished silver. "Samuel, I bless the day you bought me. That day, you spared my life and gave me hope. Today, you've given me your heart, but I give mine in return. I love you, and my only regret is that there are only twelve spokes on that spinning wheel!"

epilogue

"Here's your book, Mama."

"Thank you, Hester. I know I saw a recipe in here for pigeons." Garnet flipped through *The Art of Cookery, Made Plain and Easy*. It was the first book Samuel bought for her when he was teaching her to read better, and she treasured it.

"I can scarce believe Ethan netted this many pigeons. Hasn't he read *Poor Richard Improved* where Benjamin Franklin says, 'Kill no more pigeons than you can eat'?" Hester put the last handful of feathers into a bucket and laid a cloth across the top of it so they wouldn't blow away.

"Here we are, 'Piceons in a Hole'." Garnet struggled to rise, and Hester pulled on her arm to help. "Thank you. Let's get these made."

Hester led her into the keeping room.

" 'Take your Pigeons, season them with beaten Mace, Pepper and Salt; put a little Piece of Butter in the Belly,' " Garnet read aloud. " 'Lay them in a Dish and pour a light Batter all over them, make with a Quart of Mik and Eggs, and four or five Sploonfuls of Flour; bake it, and sent it to Table. It is a good Dish.' It does sound tasty, don't you think?"

"Yes, but Father's going to be so eager to have the pumpkin custard that he probably won't notice anything you put on the table before it." Hester lifted five-year-old Prudence onto the small chest. "You did a nice job washing your hands, so you may help us cook."

Eight-year-old Molly set aside her sampler. "Mama, I finished stitching the alphabet. Do I get to help cook, too?"

"First have a care that you put the needle back in the case. Christopher was sore mad when he stepped on the last one you lost."

"I already did." Molly looked at the pigeons. "It's good Ethan netted so many. Those look dreadfully small. Is it greedy if I eat one all by myself?"

"You and Prudence will share one." Garnet smiled at Hester. "I expect we'll have a few guests by supper time."

"Oh, merry!" Prudence clapped her hands. "It's been forever since you and Goodwife Morton and Goodman Brooks played music for us all!"

"Prudy," Molly gave her little sister an exasperated look. "That's not what Mama meant."

Prudence's lower lip stuck out in a pout. "I like Goodwife Morton. Why can't she come?"

Hester let out a trill of laughter. "She'll be here, but she's coming to help Mama."

"Mama, we'll help you." Prudence copied Molly and put a nubbin of butter inside a pigeon. "Father told us to be sure to help you lots."

"And you—" Garnet went silent as the next contraction hit.

Prudence turned to her. "Did you forget what you planned to say again?"

"She's probably thinking about how we need more butter. This is the last of what we have."

Garnet let out a shaky breath. "Yes, well, I suppose I'll take care of making more butter." She sat in the rocking chair Sam and Christopher had made for her right after she'd had Molly. "Ethan put the cream in the churn just awhile ago."

Having read how Benjamin Franklin devised an attachment that went from his wife's rocking chair to the butter churn, Samuel delighted in finding the diagram and making one for Garnet.

As she set her chair in motion and thereby started churning butter, Garnet smiled at her daughters. "Molly and Prudence, while Hester puts the pigeons in to bake, the two of you go on out to the garden and fill a bucket with peas, then sit in the shade and shell them."

"I like buttered peas," Molly said.

Ethan leaned against the doorjamb. "So do I. Mama knows it's my favorite song."

"Silly!" Prudence giggled. "We're talking 'bout supper."

Still wearing a rakish smile, Ethan looked at her. "I remember the last time you made pigeons. They tasted—"

Garnet held her breath and rocked a little faster as the next pain washed over her.

Ethan's grin fled as he bolted straight up. "Does Father know?"

"No." Garnet barely managed to squeeze out that word before the pain crested.

" 'Course Father doesn't know we're having buttered peas." Prudence scratched her little nose. "Mama just decided."

Hester set the pigeons to bake, then decided. "You girls can go to Aunt Dorcas's house to pick the peas."

"Let's hurry! Christopher gives us piggyback rides!"

Ethan grabbed two-year-old Jane. "I'll take them over and fetch Biddie Laswell." He lifted Prudence. "Molly, I'm racing you. I have longer legs, but my arms are full."

Hester shook her head as they left. "Ten years ago, I wouldn't have dreamed I'd be glad to send children to Aunt Dorcas's."

"No one is beyond the love of God." Garnet smiled. "Your father was wise enough not to revile the Ryders when they wronged him." Erasmus hadn't changed his heart until he lay on his deathbed, but Dorcas had committed her heart to the Lord and her hands to doing good deeds. She couldn't manage the farm, so when Christopher married Mary Morton, Dorcas had invited them to her place. Instead of tobacco, wheat and corn now filled the fields.

"Garnet," Sam called from the yard.

"Yes?"

He dashed through the door and took a good, long look at her. "Hester, go fetch the midwife!"

"Ethan already said he'd bring back Biddie Laswell."

Sam didn't look reassured in the least. He cleared his throat. "Jane came so fast that Biddie didn't arrive in time. Go fetch Ruth Morton. Stay there and watch her little ones."

"Yes, Father."

He shook his finger at Garnet. "I should have figured out why you sent Andrew and Titus over to the Mortons' today."

"Samuel, you're the one who said they could go with Falcon and Thomas to pick out a sturgeon." Garnet bit her lip and rocked faster. When the contraction ended, she muttered, "I'm not going to be able to help salt down the behemoth when they return."

"I can do that, Mama."

Samuel started washing his hands. "Hester, enough talk. Make haste and fetch Ruth." He dried his big, capable hands and came toward her. "Let's put you to bed."

Garnet shook her head.

"What are you looking at?"

She let out a shaky breath. "The spinning wheel. A child

for each spoke, remember?"

"Yes, but—"

"Chris, Ethan, Hester, Andrew. . . Remember how disappointed Hester was that she didn't get a sister when I had Andrew, then Titus?" Her voice died out as the next pain washed over her.

Sam let out a strained chuckle. "You made up for that with Molly, Prudence, and Jane."

Garnet reached over and held fast to his hand. "Bartholomew and Anne." They'd lost those two in their infancy.

"We loved them for the time the Lord granted them to us." Sam cupped her cheek. "God has blessed us again with this little one. Think on that."

Her hold on his hand tightened. As the pain subsided, Garnet rasped, "A child for each spoke. There's not one little one this time, Sam. Biddie told me 'tis twins."

"Twins!" His flummoxed expression wore off; then he rasped, "And you waited until now to tell me?"

"You hover and fret each time my days are accomplished and I'm to have a babe. Had we told you, you'd have been impossible."

"We've not prepared for two babes!"

"I have." She scooted to the edge of the rocking chair. "The butter will have to wait."

"This is no time to discuss churning butter! We need a second cradle." While he fretted, he helped her rise.

Garnet leaned into his warmth and strength. "They've shared a womb, Sam. They'll share the cradle just as happily." Another pain started, but the sensation shifted dramatically.

Sam swept her into his arms and laid her on their bed. "Ruth—"

"Won't be here in time." She gasped and grabbed for him. "These babes are coming faster than I thought!"

Fifteen minutes later, Sam wrapped their second baby in a blanket and sank onto the edge of the bed. "Healthy sons. Both of them. God be praised."

"Indeed, He's blessed us." Garnet accepted her other baby from him. "Two more things, though."

"What?"

"Take the pigeons out of the fire in about five minutes."

"I can do that. What else?"

"Either you explain to Hester why we now have more boys than girls, or you'd better figure out how to add another spoke to the spinning wheel!"

A Letter To Our Readers

Dear Reader:

In order that we might better contribute to your reading enjoyment, we would appreciate your taking a few minutes to respond to the following questions. We welcome your comments and read each form and letter we receive. When completed, please return to the following:

Fiction Editor
Heartsong Presents
PO Box 719
Uhrichsville, Ohio 44683

1. Did you enjoy reading *Spoke of Love* by Cathy Marie Hake?
   ❏ Very much! I would like to see more books by this author!
   ❏ Moderately. I would have enjoyed it more if

   _____

   _____

   _____

2. Are you a member of **Heartsong Presents**? ❏ Yes ❏ No
   If no, where did you purchase this book? _____

   _____

3. How would you rate, on a scale from 1 (poor) to 5 (superior), the cover design? _____

4. On a scale from 1 (poor) to 10 (superior), please rate the following elements.

   _____ Heroine   _____ Plot
   _____ Hero   _____ Inspirational theme
   _____ Setting   _____ Secondary characters

5. These characters were special because? _____

_____

_____

6. How has this book inspired your life? _____

_____

_____

7. What settings would you like to see covered in future
   Heartsong Presents books? _____

_____

_____

8. What are some inspirational themes you would like to see
   treated in future books? _____

_____

_____

9. Would you be interested in reading other **Heartsong
   Presents** titles? ❏ Yes ❏ No

10. Please check your age range:
    ❏ Under 18   ❏ 18-24
    ❏ 25-34   ❏ 35-45
    ❏ 46-55   ❏ Over 55

Name _____

Occupation _____

Address _____

City, State, Zip _____

NEW MEXICO

3 stories in 1

The stories of three women, struggling with the harsh realities life has thrown their way, play out under the historic mysterious skies of Roswell, New Mexico.

Titles by author Janet Lee Barton include: *A Promise Made*, *A Place Called Home*, and *Making Amends*.

Historical, paperback, 352 pages, 5³⁄₁₆" x 8"

_____

Hearts♥ng

Presents

__HP608	*The Engagement*, K. Comeaux	__HP659	*Bayou Beginnings*, K. M. Y'Barbo
__HP611	*Faithful Traitor*, J. Stengl	__HP660	*Hearts Twice Met*, F. Chrisman
__HP612	*Michaela's Choice*, L. Harris	__HP663	*Journeys*, T. H. Murray
__HP615	*Gerda's Lawman*, L. N. Dooley	__HP664	*Chance Adventure*, K. E. Hake
__HP616	*The Lady and the Cad*, T. H. Murray	__HP667	*Sagebrush Christmas*, B. L. Etchison
__HP619	*Everlasting Hope*, T. V. Bateman	__HP668	*Duel Love*, B. Youree
__HP620	*Basket of Secrets*, D. Hunt	__HP671	*Sooner or Later*, V. McDonough
__HP623	*A Place Called Home*, J. L. Barton	__HP672	*Chance of a Lifetime*, K. E. Hake
__HP624	*One Chance in a Million*, C. M. Hake	__HP672	*Bayou Secrets*, K. M. Y'Barbo
__HP627	*He Loves Me, He Loves Me Not*,	__HP672	*Beside Still Waters*, T. V. Bateman
	R. Druten	__HP679	*Rose Kelly*, J. Spaeth
__HP628	*Silent Heart*, B. Youree	__HP680	*Rebecca's Heart*, L. Harris
__HP631	*Second Chance*, T. V. Bateman	__HP683	*A Gentlemen's Kiss*, K. Comeaux
__HP632	*Road to Forgiveness*, C. Cox	__HP684	*Copper Sunrise*, C. Cox
__HP635	*Hogtied*, L. A. Coleman	__HP687	*The Ruse*, T. H. Murray
__HP636	*Renegade Husband*, D. Mills	__HP688	*A Handful of Flowers*, C. M. Hake
__HP639	*Love's Denial*, T. H. Murray	__HP691	*Bayou Dreams*, K. M. Y'Barbo
__HP640	*Taking a Chance*, K. E. Hake	__HP692	*The Oregon Escort*, S. P. Davis
__HP643	*Escape to Sanctuary*, M. J. Conner	__HP695	*Into the Deep*, L. Bliss
__HP644	*Making Amends*, J. L. Barton	__HP696	*Bridal Veil*, C. M. Hake
__HP647	*Remember Me*, K. Comeaux	__HP699	*Bittersweet Remembrance*, G. Fields
__HP648	*Last Chance*, C. M. Hake	__HP700	*Where the River Flows*, I. Brand
__HP651	*Against the Tide*, R. Druten	__HP703	*Moving the Mountain*, Y. Lehman
__HP652	*A Love So Tender*, T. V. Batman	__HP704	*No Buttons or Beaux*, C. M. Hake
__HP655	*The Way Home*, M. Chapman	__HP707	*Mariah's Hope*, M. J. Conner
__HP656	*Pirate's Prize*, L. N. Dooley	__HP708	*The Prisoner's Wife*, S. P. Davis

Great Inspirational Romance at a Great Price!

Heartsong Presents books are inspirational romances in contemporary and historical settings, designed to give you an enjoyable, spirit-lifting reading experience. You can choose wonderfully written titles from some of today's best authors like Peggy Darty, Sally Laity, DiAnn Mills, Colleen L. Reece, Debra White Smith, and many others.

When ordering quantities less than twelve, above titles are $2.97 each.
Not all titles may be available at time of order.

HEARTSONG
PRESENTS

If you love Christian romance…

$10.99

You'll love Heartsong Presents' inspiring and faith-filled romances by today's very best Christian authors. . .DiAnn Mills, Wanda E. Brunstetter, and Yvonne Lehman, to mention a few!

When you join Heartsong Presents, you'll enjoy four brand-new, mass market, 176-page books—two contemporary and two historical—that will build you up in your faith when you discover God's role in every relationship you read about!

Imagine. . .four new romances every four weeks—with men and women like you who long to meet the one God has chosen as the love of their lives…all for the low price of $10.99 postpaid.

Mass Market 176 Pages

To join, simply visit www.heartsong presents.com or complete the coupon below and mail it to the address provided.